The Body in the Boathouse

A SUNSET LODGE MYSTERY

DIANA XARISSA

Copyright © 2022 DX Dunn, LLC
Cover Copyright © 2022 Tell-Tale Book Covers

ISBN: 9798365120372
All Rights Reserved

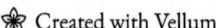 Created with Vellum

Chapter One

"Maybe this isn't a good time," the man in the doorway said hesitantly.

Abigail Clark put her hand on the top of the ladder and then slowly turned to face him. "Hi," she replied. The new arrival was an older man, at least sixty in Abigail's estimation. He was wearing jeans and a sweatshirt stretched over a rounded tummy. Both items looked as if they hadn't seen the inside of a washing machine in some time. Thick gray hair matched the long beard that gave him the appearance of a disreputable Santa.

He looked around the room and then back at her. "Someone told me you were looking for me."

Abigail frowned and then put her paintbrush in the can of paint that was precariously balanced on the rung above her. She picked up the can and then slowly climbed down the ladder. "Sorry, I can't talk from up there. Someone told you that I was looking for you?"

The man shrugged. "If you're the new owner of Sunset Lodge, then yeah. That's what I was told."

"I'm Abigail Clark. I am the new owner of Sunset Lodge.

My sister and I bought it a few months ago. We were going to run it together, but she ended up staying in New York City for the time being."

Abigail started to hold out a hand and then realized that she was covered in paint. She tried to cover the aborted gesture by reaching up to tuck a stray strand of hair behind her ear. The hair tie that she'd used to pull back her shoulder-length bob this morning wasn't doing a great job keeping her hair in place. Not that it mattered, as her light brown hair was undoubtedly covered in off-white paint now.

"I'm Barry," the man replied.

"Barry?" Abigail echoed.

"Barry Cuda."

"Oh, the boat guy," Abigail said as she finally remembered what she'd been told. "Someone told me that you used to manage the boat rentals for the Xanzibar Hotel."

Barry nodded. "That was a long time ago, though. The Xanzibar's been shut for decades."

"I was told you worked for Scott Wright for a while, too," Abigail said, trying to remember who had told her about Barry.

"I did," Barry replied flatly, a scowl momentarily flashing across his face.

Abigail hesitated. "The thing is, I'm doing everything I can to get the lodge back up and running. Jack and Janet Johnstone, the previous owners, stopped doing boat rentals years ago, but as we're right on Foxglove Lake, I'd love to be able to start offering them again."

"Could work. No one else is doing boat rentals right now. Scott Wright used to do them, but he stopped a few years back because he wasn't making enough money off of them. Some things aren't about money, though. Kids around here used to get to grow up on the lake. There were rowboats and canoes and pedal boats, all for rent. Kids could fish or just row out into the lake and have a picnic. Problem is insurance is expensive, at least according to Scott Wright."

Abigail frowned. "I hadn't thought of that. I'll have to make a few phone calls, I guess. I don't have a lot of extra money in the budget for insurance." *Or anything else at this point,* she added silently.

"So why were you looking for me?"

"It was suggested that you might be interested in running the boat rentals for me."

Barry shrugged and then scratched his head. "Maybe. I'm semi-retired now, but it might be fun to spend some time on the lake, renting out boats and fishing in between customers."

"Of course, the first thing we need to do is figure out if we actually have any boats or not."

"You don't know? What did Jack and Janet tell you?"

"That they'd locked up several canoes and pedal boats in the boathouse at the end of the summer season about ten years ago and then simply never bothered to open the boathouse again."

Barry frowned. "Someone could have stolen everything they had. If it's all still there, it could be in terrible condition."

"Mandy, that's my sister, and I walked down to the boathouse when we took our first tour of the property, but it was padlocked shut. Jack couldn't find the key for the padlock, so we never got to look inside."

"What made you and your sister decide to buy Sunset Lodge, then? You said she's in New York City?"

"She is," Abigail agreed. "We were both there until a few months ago. I was managing a small boutique hotel with a gourmet restaurant attached, and she was working two jobs she hated while hoping to land her dream job. We'd always talked about buying a business together one day, and when Mandy saw a listing for Sunset Lodge somewhere, she suggested that we seriously consider buying it."

"But then she stayed behind?"

"Just before we were due to move here, she was offered that dream job. She'd studied technical theater in college, and she was offered a chance to design sets for a production that is only just off-Broadway. It could lead to bigger and better things, or it could be her one chance to do what she's always wanted to do before she comes here and helps run Sunset Lodge for the rest of her life."

"And that leaves you on your own to run it for now."

"Yeah, and it's a big job, but I have a lot of help, too."

"Is Marcia still in the kitchen?"

Abigail nodded. "I kept everyone who was working here when we bought the lodge." Marcia Burton had been cooking breakfast and dinner for lodge guests for over twenty years.

"You kept Catastrophe Carl?"

"'Catastrophe Carl?'"

Barry laughed. "Carl Young has been the lodge's general handyman for years and years. He probably started working here before you were even born. He got the nickname when he tried his hand at some electrical work and nearly blew up the entire town. He's a decent handyman, though, as long as you don't need him to do anything electrical."

"He's still here."

"I'm surprised he isn't on the ladder, doing the painting for you."

"He's been painting the guest rooms," she explained. "And having extra days off as well. I'm trying to give everyone time off while we don't have any guests."

"It's October. I can't imagine you'll have any guests between now and May."

"Actually, we have several guests arriving toward the end of the month," Abigail replied, trying not to sound smug. "We advertised a special Halloween weekend getaway and filled all of the rooms that we currently have available."

"A Halloween getaway? What does that involve?"

"Mandy is working out the details, but basically we're going to decorate the lodge and have pumpkin carving and apple bobbing and that sort of thing. Marcia is putting together a special menu for the weekend, and I'm trying to find someone to tell ghost stories around the fire and take people on hayrides."

"I may be able to help you there."

"With the ghost stories or the hayrides?"

"Both, although I was thinking more of the ghost stories. I belong to the Nightshade Players. We're a group of actors who get together occasionally to put on a play or maybe a musical if we're feeling especially ambitious. It's been a few years since we did much of anything, but years ago we used to put together a haunted house every October. I'm sure some of us still have costumes that mostly fit. We could take turns coming up and wandering around the lodge, scaring people, if you want. Otherwise, we could just come and tell ghost stories and add atmosphere to the place."

"I don't think I want you to scare anyone, but a few ghouls or ghosts wandering around would definitely add atmosphere. I'm not sure I have the budget for that, though."

Barry shrugged. "I can't speak for everyone, but I'd be happy to come up for a few hours one day just for the fun of it. It's been a long time since I've had an excuse to dress up – not that I need one."

"Can you talk to the rest of the group about it, or should I call someone?"

"I can talk to everyone. I'll call Neal later and let him organize it. He loves to be in charge."

"Have him call me, then," she suggested. She was only a few steps away from the reception desk. There, she grabbed one of her business cards and held it out to the man. "He can call me anytime."

Barry glanced at the card and then slipped it into his pocket. "Does Arnold still work here?"

"Arnold Nagel? He's our night manager."

"His wife, Karen, did a show with us once. We tried to talk Arnold into being in it too, because there was a perfect part for a man who pumps iron all day, but he wasn't interested. He said he couldn't make it to rehearsals because of his hours here."

"He works behind the desk late every night and again very early in the morning, and he's on call in between those sessions," Abigail replied. "I can't imagine when he'd have time to rehearse for a play."

Barry shrugged. "Joe took the part. He looks like a body-builder – in his own mind, at least."

Abigail laughed. "I'm starting to look forward to meeting the rest of the Nightshade Players."

"I'm sure they'll be happy to do something. As I said, it's been a while."

"I can't pay much," Abigail warned him.

"We never got paid in the past. Any money we made from ticket sales always went back into the group to pay for costumes and props and sets for the next show." He paused and then laughed. "We used to have a party on the last night of the show, too. That was always paid for out of ticket sales too, which usually meant that we ended up with only a few dollars left for whatever we needed for the next show."

"If I don't have to pay you, I'd be more than happy to feed you all when you're here. As I said, Marcia is going to be putting together a special menu for the weekend. She can easily cook for a few extra people."

"I won't say no to that," Barry replied. "I love Marcia's cooking, and I don't get to have it very often. She always brings the best dishes to the Christmas Festival."

"Christmas Festival?"

"You haven't heard about the Nightshade Christmas Festival yet?"

Abigail shook her head.

"It's an annual tradition, started years and years ago. Actually, I think it was probably started by Herb and Tammy Fuhrman back during the month or two that they owned the Xanzibar. It was called the Nightshade Hotel in those days, and they started the Nightshade Christmas Festival to help attract guests to the hotel in December."

"And the festival continued even after they'd sold the hotel?"

"The festival didn't even start until after they'd sold the hotel," he laughed. "As I said earlier, they only owned the hotel for a month or two. It opened in June or July, and they'd sold it by the end of August, I think. I was managing the boat rentals for them, but they didn't say anything to anyone about the sale, not before or after. The first we knew about it was when we got our paychecks from somewhere else."

"Wow."

"We didn't know what to make of it, but we'd all been given a small raise, so none of us complained," he remembered.

"And then you had the first Christmas Festival?"

"Oh, yeah, that's what we were talking about. Yeah, Tammy had been planning this big Christmas Festival, and even after the hotel was sold, she kept on planning. The event has changed a lot since then, of course, but it's still a big thing for Nightshade."

"What happens at the Christmas Festival now, then?"

"Well, for a start, it's now called the Nightshade Winter Festival," Barry replied with a scowl. "Scott Wright is the main sponsor now, and he insisted that we change the name to be more inclusive, whatever that means. They set up a half dozen huge tents across the baseball and soccer fields at the town park. Scott pays to have big heaters put in every tent, which is why he gets to name the event. I suppose I should be grateful he hasn't renamed it the Wright Festival or something like that."

Abigail grinned. "And what happens in all of the tents?"

"One will be full of people selling crafty stuff. Another is more like a yard sale. It takes place the week before Christmas, so both tents are really popular. There's one tent full of cookies and other baked goods. Another has carnival-type games, including everyone's favorite dunk tank. The high school principal and a few other notable folks from around town each take a turn at the dunk tank."

"It all sounds like fun."

"For a small town like Nightshade, it's a big deal. If you like that sort of thing, though, you should drive over to Ramsey. They have events like that every single month."

"Really? I may have to check out some of them. Is this the only event that happens in Nightshade?"

"Nah, there's a fair in the summer and an apple festival in the fall, too. The Christmas Festival is the best, though."

Abigail nodded. "I wonder if people outside of Nightshade would be interested in our Christmas, er, Winter Festival. I'm going to have to find out more about it."

"Talk to Scott Wright. He's in charge. If he likes you, he'll probably let you make lots of changes to it as well."

"I don't want to change anything. I just want to figure out the best way to promote the event to potential guests."

Barry's eyes narrowed slightly. "I reckon you and Scott will get along just fine," he muttered.

Feeling as if she'd angered the man, Abigail changed the subject. "But we were talking about boats," she said. "I assume the lake freezes over in the winter months?"

"Yeah, lots of people go out ice fishing, and Scott sets up an ice rink near the center of town."

"So we won't be able to start renting out boats until spring."

He nodded. "And you probably won't find many people interested in going out on the lake until late spring. It can still feel quite cold on the lake in April."

"So if we were going to advertise boating, it would be for the summer months," Abigail said, mostly talking to herself.

"June, July, and August," Barry agreed. "Maybe September, but it rains a lot in September. The kind of folks who rent rowboats or pedal boats to splash around Foxglove Lake for an hour or two aren't going to bother in the rain."

Abigail nodded. "I'm not sure it will be worth the time and effort to reopen the boathouse."

"We should probably start by seeing what's down there. If you wanted to open this summer, you may need to start ordering parts or even replacement boats."

"Yes, that's a good point. Do you have time now to take a look?"

Barry shrugged. "I don't have anything else to do."

Wishing she could say the same, Abigail picked up her paint can. "Give me a minute to clean up and we'll go and see what we can find."

There was a utility sink in the large room next to the kitchen. It also housed two industrial-sized washing machines and dryers. Abigail rinsed her brush and then wrapped it in plastic wrap. "I'll be back for you soon," she told the brush as she put it on a nearby shelf. After replacing the lid on the paint can, she spent several minutes scrubbing her hands and lower arms, trying to remove as much paint as possible. A quick look in the mirror by the door showed her that her face and hair were both covered in splatters and spots of beige paint.

"It doesn't matter," she muttered as she walked back toward the lobby.

"What doesn't matter?" Marcia asked from inside the kitchen.

Abigail laughed. "I'm a mess. I wouldn't normally go outside looking like this, but Barry is here, so we're going to walk down to the boathouse and see what Jack and Janet left behind."

Marcia made a face. "I can't imagine you'll find much that's still seaworthy. That boathouse has been locked up tight for ten years or more."

"Maybe Barry can use all of the parts from what's down there to make at least one or two useable boats. It would be a start, at least."

"Good luck," Marcia told her.

When Abigail reached the lobby, Barry was sitting in front of the fireplace, his legs stretched out in front of him. His eyes were closed, and as she approached him she realized that he was snoring quietly. As she tried to work out the best way to wake him, she thought about keys. Jack and Janet had told her that they hadn't been able to find the key to the padlock on the boathouse door, but it was still probably worth taking the ring of keys that they had given her. They might have been mistaken.

She went into the office and pulled out the large ring of keys. It was helpfully labeled "Miscellaneous Keys." Slamming the desk drawer shut, she clomped loudly back into the lobby.

Barry opened one eye. "I hear yah," he muttered.

Abigail crossed to the door as he slowly got to his feet.

"I'm not sure why the boathouse is so far away," she said as they began to follow the path from the lodge toward the lake.

"I was told that Jack's dad, when he had the boathouse built, didn't want to block the views of the lake from the main building," Barry told her. "He thought the boathouse was unsightly."

The path led directly to the lake. A second path ran along

the edge of the lake before disappearing into a cluster of trees, shrubs, and long grass.

"You're going to need to have someone clear this path," Barry remarked as Abigail tried to stomp down the tall grass.

"It's farther than I remembered," she muttered as the path went around a curve and then headed back toward the lake. "And uglier," she added when the boathouse came into view.

Barry laughed. "It's just a shack, really, but it wouldn't take much effort to improve it. You could paint it, for a start. It looks as if it needs a new roof, too."

Abigail sighed. "We should have taken a closer look at this before we bought the lodge. I can't afford to put a new roof on this place, not right away."

"I can probably patch what's up there. Don't give up yet," Barry told her. "Let's see how bad it is inside first."

Long grass and thick sand made the last part of the walk to the door difficult. There, two steps led up to a battered wooden porch. Abigail looked at the padlock and then at her keys.

"I don't think any of these are the right size for this lock," she said. Two minutes later, she'd checked every key. None of them fit. "We're going to need bolt cutters or something," she said with a sigh.

Barry shook his head. "It's a cheap padlock. I can pick it."

"Pick it?" Abigail echoed.

He looked at the lock and then back at her. "It doesn't look all that old, really. This hasn't been here for ten years."

She was surprised when Barry pulled a small pouch out of his pocket. He pulled a few thin tools out of the pouch and then went to work on the lock. Less than a minute later, he grinned at her.

"Easy as pie," he said as the lock opened. He removed it from the door and then slid back the bar that was holding the door shut.

"There isn't any power down here. We should have brought a flashlight," Abigail said as Barry pulled the door open.

He chuckled and then returned his lock picks to their case and put them in his pocket. When he pulled his hand out again, he was holding a small flashlight.

"It's pretty bright, especially for its size," he said as he switched it on.

"It smells terrible in there," Abigail said as she took a step forward.

"There are probably animals making the building their home."

Abigail shuddered as Barry shined the flashlight into one corner of the space.

"That's a rowboat," he said, slowly moving the light from left to right. "And another one. And a pedal boat, or what's left of one. And that's a skeleton in another rowboat."

Abigail swallowed hard as the light came to rest on the skeleton that appeared to be lying in the rowboat.

Chapter Two

"It must be an old Halloween decoration," Barry said. "Right?"

Abigail inhaled slowly. "Maybe. But maybe not. We need to call the police. It will be up to them to figure out what we've found."

Barry looked as if he wanted to argue, but after a moment, he shrugged. "And that's another pedal boat," he said, moving the light again. "And another one. I count three of each, then, including the rowboat with the skeleton."

Trying to keep her hands from shaking, Abigail dug into her pocket to find her cell phone.

"What is your emergency?" The voice on the phone sounded a lot calmer than Abigail felt.

"We found a skeleton," she replied.

"Tell her it could just be a Halloween decoration," Barry suggested.

"It could just be a Halloween decoration," she parroted.

"But it might not be?" the 911 operator asked.

"I don't know, but I don't want to go in and take a better look, just in case."

"Go in where? Where are you?"

"I'm at the boathouse," Abigail replied before taking a deep breath. "Sorry, this is Abigail Clark at Sunset Lodge. Barry and I came down to see what we could find in the boathouse. I've been thinking about trying to rent boats again this summer. When we opened the door, we found a skeleton lying in one of the boats."

"So you need the police. I'll send someone right away. Please don't go into the boathouse."

"I have no intention of going into the boathouse," Abigail assured her. "Not today, and maybe never."

"The nearest officer is on his way."

"Great," Abigail replied. "We'll just walk back up to the lodge to watch for him. There isn't any way to drive down to the boathouse." She ended the call and dropped the phone back into her pocket.

"It was probably Jack's idea of a joke," Barry said as the pair began the walk back. "He probably thought it would be funny if Janet went down to the boathouse for something and found a skeleton in one of the boats."

"It's not funny," Abigail replied flatly.

Barry nodded. "I'd really appreciate it if you didn't tell the police exactly how we got the padlock off the door," he said in a low voice.

"But if I tell them that I unlocked it, they'll want the key. And we don't want to tell them that the lock was unlocked, not if that really is a dead body in there."

Barry sighed. "I'm going to get into some trouble for having lock picks," he explained.

"Tell them they're mine," she replied impulsively. "I'll tell them that Jack had left them in the desk in case I needed them."

"Do you know how to use lock picks?"

"Nope."

THE BODY IN THE BOATHOUSE

"I could teach you some day. It isn't hard."

"That's a scary thought."

They stopped when they reached the front of the main lodge building and sat together on the small bench near the road.

"You found Rusty Morris, didn't you?" Barry asked after a moment.

Abigail nodded. "It was horrible."

"I think I might know who we found back there."

"I thought you said it was just a Halloween decoration."

"I hope it is, but I sort of recognized the jacket that was hanging on the wall behind the boat."

"The jacket? Behind the boat? There was a jacket hanging on the wall behind the boat?" Abigail shut her eyes and tried to remember what she'd seen. It was no use. As soon as Barry had said the word skeleton, she'd closed her eyes and turned away before she'd had a chance to do anything more than get a glimpse of what he'd seen.

"Yeah, and one I recognized."

"Was it something unusual? Lots of people can own the same jacket."

Barry frowned. "If I'm right, this jacket was one of a kind. A woman I used to know made it herself."

"Used to know?" Abigail echoed.

"She sort of disappeared," he replied, stumbling over his words. "I mean, she, we, I..."

As he trailed off, Abigail patted his arm. "Why don't you wait and tell all of this to the police."

Barry blinked several times. "It can't be Helena. It just can't. Maybe she set the whole thing up to surprise Jack and Janet. I can see her doing that. She has a wicked sense of humor. She probably hung up her jacket while she was setting up the fake skeleton and then just forgot to put it back on."

Abigail swallowed a dozen replies, struggling to find words

that would be appropriate under the circumstances. "How long has it been since you've seen your friend?" she asked eventually.

"About five years," Barry replied with a shrug. "I wasn't keeping track or anything. One day she was there and then one day she wasn't. We were, um, good friends, but we didn't live in each other's pockets."

"If she did set up the skeleton to surprise Jack and Janet, I wonder why she thought they'd be going into the boathouse once she'd done it," Abigail said, her mind racing. "It had already been locked up for five years by that point, hadn't it?"

"Yeah, yeah, and that's a good point. What was Helena doing in the boathouse?"

Getting herself killed, Abigail thought. She bit her tongue and then sighed. "The police sure are taking their time."

"I suppose skeletons don't rate the same sort of response as newly dead bodies."

Abigail shuddered. "They seemed to take forever that day, too."

"Maybe Helena gave the jacket to someone," Barry said, staring at the path to the lake. "Maybe that someone broke into the boathouse and then had a heart attack or something."

"There are lots of possibilities," Abigail replied in a measured tone.

"I suppose Helena could have had a heart attack in the boathouse, but I can't imagine why she would have gone in there in the first place."

"The police are here," Abigail said, jumping up as soon as the marked car turned down the short driveway that led to the small parking lot behind the lodge.

"Good afternoon," Trooper Greg Trushell said as he emerged from his car.

"Good afternoon," Abigail replied.

"I was told you think you may have found a dead body."

THE BODY IN THE BOATHOUSE

She shrugged. "It's just a skeleton, or rather, that's all that I could see from the doorway using a flashlight. As soon as I saw it, I closed my eyes and walked away. It may well be just an old Halloween decoration, though. Maybe we should have taken a better look before we called you."

"I took a better look," Barry said flatly.

Abigail jumped. She hadn't realized that the man had followed her into the parking lot.

"And?" Greg asked.

"And it looked a lot like a real skeleton, and behind it was a jacket that I recognized."

The state trooper frowned. "You recognized a jacket that was near the skeleton?"

Barry nodded. "One of my friends makes all of her own clothing. The jacket in the boathouse is one that I think she made."

Greg pulled out a notebook and pen. "Her name?"

"Helena Lane."

"She moved away a few years back, didn't she?" Greg asked.

"About five years ago," Barry agreed.

Greg looked up from his notes. "Where did she go?"

"I don't know," Barry said in a low voice. "She didn't tell me she was leaving. We'd been fighting a bit more than usual, so I wasn't surprised when she didn't come over to my place for a few days. Before I went looking for her, someone told me that she'd left town."

"Interesting," Greg said. "And you think one of her jackets is hanging in the boathouse?"

"I'd need a closer look to be sure, but it looked like one of hers. The fabric is quite unusual," Barry replied.

Greg opened his trunk and pulled out a large flashlight. "I'm going to go and see what I can see," he told them. "I'd appreciate it if you'd wait here. Please don't call or text anyone for the time being."

Abigail and Barry both nodded and then followed the man back toward the path to the lake.

"The path to the boathouse is pretty overgrown," Abigail said apologetically as she stopped at the bench where they'd been sitting earlier.

"What did Jack and Janet tell you about the boathouse?" Greg asked.

"They just said that they'd stopped doing boat rentals about ten years ago. They said there were a few old boats in the boathouse, but that they couldn't guarantee that any of them would still be useable," she replied.

"Ten years ago?" Greg checked.

Abigail nodded.

"I remember Helena being in shows more recently than that," Greg said to Barry.

"Yeah, she left town about five years ago," he replied.

"I assume the building was locked in some way." Greg looked at Abigail.

"There was a padlock on the door. Jack couldn't find the key for it, but I had a set of lock picks, and we used them to open the lock."

"You just happen to have had a set of lock picks?" Greg looked skeptical.

"A friend of mine gave them to me one year for my birthday. We were in a book club together, and we'd read this story about a thief who used lock picks. My friend got everyone in the group a cheap set of them for Christmas that year."

"I thought you said he gave them to you for your birthday," Greg replied.

Abigail felt her cheeks burn. *I'm a terrible liar*, she thought as she tried to think of how to save the situation.

"They're my lock picks," Barry said with a sigh. "When I

THE BODY IN THE BOATHOUSE

arranged to meet with Abigail, she mentioned that she didn't have the key to the padlock on the boathouse and asked if I had bolt cutters. I offered to bring my lock picks to see if I could get the lock open."

Greg frowned at Abigail. "So you were lying?"

"I didn't want to get Barry into any trouble. He was kind enough to bring his lock picks and open the lock for me, after all," she told him.

"All of this will be in my report to the detective who investigates," Greg replied.

"There may not be anything to investigate," Abigail said. "I'm still hoping it's just a Halloween decoration."

Greg stared at her for a minute and then shrugged. "Did you put the padlock back on the door?"

"No. When we opened it, we hung it open on the door," Abigail said. "We did shut the door, but we didn't lock the padlock again."

"I'll be right back. As I said, no phones, please."

Abigail sat down on the bench and sighed deeply.

"You're a terrible liar," Barry said as he sat down next to her. "Thanks for trying, but next time, just tell me that you can't lie to save your life. It would have saved us both some trouble."

"I'm sorry. I didn't want you to be in any trouble, but I knew I was going to mess things up when I tried to claim the lock picks as mine."

Barry shrugged. "Don't worry about it. If things go the way I think they're going to go, Greg is going to have bigger concerns."

"You think that the skeleton is real?"

"I do. I just hope it isn't Helena."

"You said she makes her own clothes?"

"Yeah. Some, anyway, not everything. She used to make a lot of the costumes for our shows, too. She's really talented."

"She was part of the Nightshade Players?"

"Yeah, when she was here."

"Was she from Nightshade?"

Barry shook his head. "She grew up in the south somewhere. I forget exactly where. Georgia, I think, but she left as soon as she turned eighteen. Her father was a mean drunk, and her mother wasn't around much. Helena got herself through school and then, the day after she graduated, she hit the road."

"Was she an only child?"

"Yeah, apparently her mother used to tell her that she wasn't so dumb that she'd make the same mistake twice whenever Helena used to say she wanted a brother or a sister."

Abigail frowned. "What a horrible thing to say to your child."

"Like I said, Helena got out as soon as she could."

"How old was she when she came to Nightshade?"

"Somewhere in her fifties. I was never foolish enough to ask," Barry told her with a small grin.

"What brought her to Nightshade?"

Barry shrugged. "Nothing. Life. Happenstance, maybe. She never stays in one place for more than a few years. She likes to move around, have new experiences, see new things. By the time she got here, she'd already been all the way across the country and back three times. She used to tell me stories about the things she'd seen out west. She lived in Las Vegas for three years, which was the longest she'd ever stayed anywhere. She said it was the most interesting place she'd ever lived and that she wanted to go back one day. It was the only place in the country that she wanted to revisit, and she'd been to lots of places."

"What did she do for a living?"

"She used to wait tables, mostly. In Vegas, she worked in one of the casinos, dealing blackjack. She told me that some of the high rollers used to tip her really well. She managed to build up a little nest egg while she was there."

"What did she do while she was here?"

"She worked for Peter down at the Nightshade Diner," he replied, naming a local diner that Abigail knew was open twenty-four hours a day, seven days a week. "He was upset when she left because she'd been his most popular waitress."

"And she was part of your theater group?"

"Yeah, that's where I met her. She saw a sign for auditions and decided to try out for a part in a show. We were getting ready to do *The March of the Myst Toad.*"

"I don't think I've ever heard of that."

"No one has ever heard of it," Barry replied. "It was written by one of our local playwrights. Believe it or not, Nightshade is home to three different playwrights. Actually, it's only two now, because Stanley passed away a few years ago. He kindly left his entire body of work to the Players, so that we can perform his shows forever."

"How nice," Abigail said, trying not to sound doubtful.

Barry laughed. "It isn't as if anyone else would have wanted them. They're uniformly terrible, his plays. *The March of the Myst Toad* was one of his, and it was pretty awful, but Stanley managed to persuade Neal that the play had the perfect part for him, and Neal managed to persuade the rest of us to give Stanley's story a chance."

"How was the show, then?"

"We never made it out of rehearsals. First, we struggled to cast it. Not many actors are interested in playing the part of an overweight, middle-aged toad with a broken leg and bad breath."

"The main character was supposed to be an actual toad?"

Barry nodded. "A myst toad, M – Y – S – T, which was supposed to explain why he was human-sized and could speak."

"Okay," Abigail said, wishing she'd never started this part of the conversation.

"Anyway, we finally found a high school kid who was willing to take the part, but by that time we were already two weeks behind schedule. Helena had to work on the costumes, but she really struggled with the toad costume. It wasn't her fault. Stanley had this idea in his head of exactly how the toad should look, but we didn't have the budget or the expertise to meet his expectations. The sets were another problem." Barry sighed and shook his head.

"So it never actually got performed?"

"We canceled the whole thing about two weeks before the show was supposed to open. We'd only sold a handful of tickets, mostly to Stanley's family."

"He must have been disappointed."

"By the time we canceled, I think he was relieved. He'd hated everything that we'd done up to that point. He told me afterward that when he closed his eyes, he could see the story unfolding like a movie. His version didn't look anything like ours, and I think he was secretly happy that we never performed the show for an audience."

"Was Helena disappointed?"

"Not at all. We all went out for a few drinks to celebrate after the director pulled the plug. Helena and I stayed after the others left and kept drinking and talking until the bar closed. Then we went back to my place and, um, Helena ended up staying the night."

"I hadn't realized that you and she were a couple," Abigail murmured.

"She stayed with me for about six months, and then she decided to get her own place. At first she still stayed with me most nights, but over time she started spending more and more time in her own apartment. Then one day she simply stopped coming around at all." Barry sat forward and put his head in his hands. "She can't be dead," he muttered.

"I'm sorry," Abigail replied, patting his back gently.

"She started talking about leaving," he said after a minute. "She said she was getting bored with Nightshade, but she actually invited me to leave with her. She said that we could go anywhere, do anything, if I wanted to go along."

"What did you say?"

"I said I needed time to think about the offer. I've lived in Nightshade my entire life aside from a short stint in the Navy. Her stories about her travels were interesting, but I'd never felt tempted to do any traveling of my own, not before I met Helena. She told me that I could think for a week or two, but no longer. When I saw her again a day or two later, she didn't mention leaving. That was the last time I saw her."

"I'm going to ask you both to stop talking," Greg said loudly as he walked toward them. "I've called for a crime scene team and a detective. The detective will want to question both of you as soon as he or she arrives."

Chapter Three

"I don't know anything," Abigail said.

Greg nodded. "But the body was found on your property, in your boathouse. Obviously, you'll have to answer some questions."

"It's her, then?" Barry asked hoarsely.

"All I can tell you is that I believe the remains in the boathouse are of human origin," Greg replied. "I didn't go into the building and I'm certainly no expert on human remains, but from what I could see, I felt that a crime scene team was needed."

"So it still could be just a Halloween decoration?" Barry demanded.

Greg frowned and then nodded slowly. "It could be."

"I should try calling Helena," Barry said. "I still have her number in my phone. I really thought she'd come back one day."

He pulled out his cell phone and stared at the screen.

"Maybe you should wait to do anything until the detective gets here," Greg suggested.

"If she answers, we'll know the body isn't hers, and you

can ask her why she left her coat in the boathouse," Barry replied. After some scrolling and tapping, he held up the phone. "I put it on speaker," he said.

Abigail felt as if she was holding her breath as the phone began to ring. She counted five rings before a loud click.

Hey, this is Debbie. Leave a message, 'kay?

Barry frowned and then disconnected.

"Looks like she changed her number," Greg said.

"She always kept her cell phone in the inside pocket on the right side of that coat," Barry replied flatly. "She made the coat herself, so she added a bunch of extra pockets, and she made them all big and with ways to keep them closed. Helena hated to carry around a purse. That was one of the reasons why she'd started making her own clothes."

Abigail wondered if Barry had realized that he was now talking about the woman in the past tense. It seemed likely that Greg had noticed, even if Barry had not.

"The crime scene team will go over every inch of the boathouse and everything in it," Greg replied. "If the victim left behind a cell phone, they'll find it."

Barry opened his mouth to reply, but snapped it shut again as two cars appeared on the road in front of the lodge. They both pulled into the parking lot. Abigail swallowed a sigh as Detective Fred Williams got out of one of them.

"Ms. Clark, good afternoon," he said when he reached her.

"Call me Abigail," she replied. "I hope you won't take this the wrong way, but I was hoping I'd never see you again, not in your, um, professional capacity."

The fifty-something man chuckled. "I understand. But what's this I hear about another body at the lodge?"

"It's just a skeleton, and it's in the boathouse," Abigail replied. "It may be just a Halloween decoration or something."

"I have someone coming to make that determination,"

Fred told her. He turned to the man next to her. "Bertram Wallace, I wasn't expecting to see you here," he said, nodding.

Barry frowned. "It's Barry," he said.

"Ah, yes, you go by Barry Cuda, don't you?" Fred replied.

"No law against nicknames," Barry said defensively.

"No, of course not," Fred agreed.

"Barry thinks he might know the victim," Greg interjected.

Fred raised an eyebrow. "Is that so?"

"I didn't say that," Barry said quickly. "I just said that I thought I recognized the jacket that was hanging on the wall in the boathouse."

"Whose jacket is it?" Fred asked.

"I think it might have belonged to Helena Lane," Barry replied.

Fred pulled out a notebook and made a note. "I remember someone named Helena Lane," he said thoughtfully. "She was only in Nightshade for a year or so about five or six years ago, if I'm remembering the right woman."

"You are," Barry said grudgingly.

"I took her statement when her apartment was broken into," Fred told him.

"Her apartment was broken into? I didn't know that," Barry replied.

Fred frowned. "I'm going to have to go back through my files. I seem to remember that it happened not long after she'd moved to the area. She was renting an apartment at Sandy Shores, that complex that got torn down last year."

"They had a lot of problems with break-ins during the last ten years that they were open," Greg said. "I don't think anyone was sorry to see the building demolished."

"Some of the older residents, the ones who'd been there for decades, were pretty upset," Fred told him.

"All that must have happened before I met Helena," Barry said. "When we met, she was living in The Towers."

Fred frowned. "It's quite a step up from Sandy Shores to The Towers. She must have found a different job. When she was living at Sandy Shores, she was working for the Nightshade Diner."

Barry shrugged. "Maybe she won the lottery."

"Does anyone ever actually win the lottery?" Greg asked.

The occupants of the second car had disappeared down the path to the lake. Now one of the men reappeared.

"Fred, we need to talk," he said as he approached them.

Fred nodded and then followed the man a short distance away. After a short conversation, Fred walked back over to the bench while the other man headed toward his car.

"I'm going to need to speak to each of you individually," Fred said. "Ideally, I'd like to set up a temporary office out here to use while we process the crime scene."

"I can give you a room in the annex," Abigail offered. "2A is completely empty right now. I have tables and chairs that you can use."

"2A?" Fred repeated. "The room where the body was found last month?"

Abigail nodded. "All of the furniture was cleaned and then removed. I got rid of the bed, but everything else from the room has been stored elsewhere. The carpet was taken out and specialists cleaned the entire room. I haven't had new carpet put in yet, but the walls and ceiling were all painted in the last week or so."

"I suppose we can use that room," Fred conceded.

"All of the other rooms have beds in them," Abigail pointed out.

"We'll use 2A," Fred replied. "If you can get me a table and two chairs, I'll interview you first, and then you can get back to whatever you were doing before you found the body."

"I was painting," Abigail replied, conscious that she was still speckled in paint. "Let me get a set of keys from inside, and then I can find you some furniture for your temporary office."

When Abigail went inside, Carl, Marcia, and Arnold, the night manager, were all standing in the lobby, staring out the window at the police cars in the parking lot.

"What's going on?" Carl demanded as Abigail crossed the lobby.

"Barry and I found a skeleton in the boathouse," she replied, trying to keep her tone neutral.

"A skeleton?" Marcia repeated. "I suppose that's marginally better than a dead body."

"It's still a dead body," Abigail said flatly. "It's just one that's been there for a while."

"Was someone using the boathouse as a temporary home?" Arnold asked.

"I've no idea. It didn't look as if anyone had been staying there, though. The skeleton was the only thing that looked as if it didn't belong," Abigail told him.

"What now?" Carl asked as Abigail started going through the box of keys.

"Now the police are going to use 2A as a temporary office while they investigate. It's still possible that the skeleton is nothing but an old Halloween decoration or maybe something someone stole from the high school biology department. If we have found human remains, then the police will have a lot to investigate," she replied.

"You're putting them in 2A?" Marcia asked.

"It's empty. We can move some tables and chairs into the room for them. All of the other rooms have large beds in them," Abigail explained.

"Do you need me and Arnold to move some furniture, then?" Carl asked.

"If you guys could grab the two folding tables in the office, I'll start moving chairs from the other annex rooms into 2A. That should give them enough, I hope."

"There are some folding chairs in the basement," Carl told her.

"I'll tell Fred. He can let one of us know if they need them," she replied.

Keys in hand, she turned and headed back outside while Carl and Arnold went to find the tables she'd requested.

Fifteen minutes later, the small annex room was ready for use.

"I hate it in here," Abigail said to Fred, shuddering as she looked around the space. "This is the first time I've actually been inside the room since before I found the body in here."

Fred nodded. "I know that was traumatic for you, but the room had nothing to do with what happened."

"That makes sense in theory, but I still don't think I'll ever use it for guests again. Maybe I'll change my mind if we ever start getting busy."

"Have a seat," Fred suggested, gesturing toward the nearest chair.

Abigail sat down and then pulled the chair a bit closer to the table in front of her. Fred sat down on the opposite side of the table and then pulled out his notebook and his phone.

"I'm going to record this, if that's okay with you," he said.

She nodded. "Whatever."

He smiled sympathetically. "I know this is difficult for you. I can assure you that such events are quite unusual for Nightshade. I'm fairly certain the remains are human, but I'm hopeful that there might be an innocent explanation for what happened."

"Innocent?"

"Let's say non-criminal," Fred suggested. "It's possible

that someone was using the boathouse as a temporary shelter and simply passed away from natural causes, for example."

"Someone locked the door with the body inside."

"Perhaps," Fred said. "Although there could be other explanations for that as well. But you said something about maybe needing this room if the lodge gets busy. Does that mean that you don't have many guests at the moment?"

"I don't have any guests at the moment," Abigail told him. "I'm not actively looking for any, either, although I wouldn't turn some away if they came to the door."

"I hope things improve."

"We have guests arriving on Friday for a special Halloween weekend," she told him. "We're expecting to use all four of the guest rooms on the second floor and also two of the rooms in the annex."

"Aren't you staying in a room on the second floor?"

"I have been since the, um, incident last month, but I'll be moving back out to one of the annex rooms before our Halloween guests start to arrive. We're hoping to finish the painting on the ground floor in the next day or two. Carl has been touching up the paint in the guest rooms on the second floor, which means I've been moving around a bit, but I think he's nearly finished. The guest rooms on the higher floors are going to have to wait for November."

"And where will Arnold be staying while you have all of these guests?"

Arnold and his wife, Karen, lived in a small cottage on the edge of the lodge's property. Because he was on call throughout the night when the lodge had guests, he usually slept in an empty guest room on those nights. It was an arrangement that had worked well when Jack and Janet had owned the lodge, and Abigail didn't see any need to change it, even though she was busy trying to paint and redecorate the rooms.

"We're planning on having him stay in one of the third-floor guest rooms," she explained. "They're very dated and I wouldn't let paying guests use them, but it's better than making the poor man sleep on the couch in the office again."

Fred nodded. "What constitutes a special Halloween weekend, then?"

"Mostly, we're going to decorate the lodge so it looks slightly spooky, but still reassuringly cozy," Abigail explained. "We're going to have a pumpkin carving contest and a bonfire with apple bobbing and whatever else I can think of that's suitably autumnal. Marcia has been coming up with special menus for every meal, all themed around Halloween and fall. Barry thought he might be able to find a few local actors who would be willing to dress up and maybe tell ghost stories as well."

"How well do you know Barry?"

"I met him for the first time today. Someone suggested weeks ago that he might be interested in running summer boat rentals for me, but I had trouble tracking him down."

"Did he have an appointment to come and see you today?"

"No, not at all. He simply turned up."

Fred made a note. "Were you thinking of renting out boats for the Halloween weekend?"

"No. We were talking about trying to do something in the summer. I'd never seen inside the boathouse before today. I wasn't even sure there were actually boats in there until Barry opened the door. I still don't know what sort of condition any of them are in."

"I'm trying to understand why you suddenly went into the boathouse today," Fred said. "I don't think you even mentioned it when we talked last month."

"Getting inside the boathouse was a low priority for me, but once Barry was here, it made sense to at least take a look.

As he pointed out, if we need to order parts for the boats or even new boats, that could take some time."

"Do you know why Barry chose today to visit you?"

"I've no idea," Abigail replied, hoping she wasn't going to get Barry into trouble with her answer.

"Let's go back through your day, then," Fred said. "Tell me everything you can remember talking about with Barry before you went down to the boathouse."

Abigail did her best to repeat the conversation, but she knew she was forgetting things. "I'm sorry," she said eventually. "It didn't seem all that important at the time."

"Once you agreed to go down to the boathouse, what happened next?" Fred asked.

Sighing, she told him about their walk to the boathouse. She stumbled over her words a bit when she reached the part where Barry had pulled out his lock picks, but she got through it. "And then Barry and I walked back to the road to wait for the police," she finally concluded.

Fred had her repeat the conversations that had taken place since she'd dialed 911 and then asked her several additional questions.

"Your sister is involved in theater. I wonder if she's ever met Helena Lane," he said as he put his pen down next to his notebook.

"I can call her and ask," Abigail offered.

"I may ask you to do that if this does turn out to be a murder investigation, and we manage to identify the body."

Abigail shuddered. "I hate thinking that the skeleton has been out in the boathouse for five years or more."

"Do you have a phone number for Jack and Janet?" Fred asked as he got to his feet.

"I don't, actually. Before I bought the lodge, I simply called the number here when I had questions. I can tell you that they used Quail Duncan as their lawyer for the sale, if that helps."

"Everyone in town uses Quail when they sell or buy houses. He won't give me any information about anything, but maybe I can persuade him to tell Jack and Janet that I'd like to talk to them."

"They must have left contact information with some of their friends," Abigail suggested.

"I'm fairly certain Jessica, next door, knows how to reach them, but she's less likely to share that with me than Quail is," Fred told her. "Thank you for your time and for the use of one of your rooms. I'll come and talk to you again before the end of the day."

Abigail nodded and then got up and followed Fred out of the room.

"I just need to check on a few things," he told her as she turned to walk back to the main building. "I'll be in to get Barry in a few minutes."

"I'll tell him."

"You were out there for ages," Barry said as Abigail walked toward the bench where he was still sitting.

"I know," she replied. "Fred will be ready for you soon."

Barry frowned. "I don't want to talk to him."

Abigail glanced at the uniformed trooper who was standing next to Barry. "You do want to help him figure out what happened to the person we found in the boathouse, though, don't you?"

"If it's Helena, then yes, but otherwise, I'm not sure what I want."

"What does that mean?"

"It means whatever happened out there happened a long time ago. Maybe it's best to simply leave things alone."

"If our skeleton was murdered, I definitely want the police to investigate," Abigail said firmly.

Barry shrugged. "Helena would never hurt anyone, not on purpose."

"But if someone hurt her, you'd want that someone found, right?"

"I just want all of this to be over. I need a drink, or maybe ten."

"Me too, and I don't drink," Abigail replied.

"I drink too much," Barry told her. "Helena always said so." He leaned forward and put his head in his hands.

Abigail looked at the trooper and then back at Barry. "I'm sorry," she said softly.

She couldn't understand his muffled reply. Before she could ask him to repeat it, Fred appeared, walking up from the path to the lake.

"Barry? Let's go and have a chat," he said when he reached the bench.

Barry stood up and pressed his lips together. He nodded at Abigail and then followed Fred toward the annex. Abigail sighed and then walked the rest of the way to the lodge.

"The phone has been ringing off the hook," Carl told her as she walked into the lobby.

"I didn't think to forward it to my cell," she replied with a sigh. "Sorry about that. It doesn't usually ring very often."

"It's been nothing but reporters, trying to find out why the police are here," he said. "I keep telling them no comment, but they don't listen."

"Wonderful. Maybe we should just let all of the calls go to the answering machine."

"I was going to do that, but I was worried that we might miss a guest or two if we did that."

"That's always a worry." Abigail sighed as the phone began to ring.

"Hello?"

"Abigail, hello," a friendly voice said. "This is Ross, Ross Danielson at the *Nightshade News*. How are you today?"

"I'm fine, thank you. Busy, of course."

"Busy? Busy doing what?"

"Painting. We're painting all of the walls and ceilings on the ground floor before our exciting Halloween weekend," she explained. "And don't ask me to buy any advertising for the Halloween weekend, as we don't have room for any additional guests."

"That may change, though, once your guests find out about the dead body, don't you think?"

"Dead body?" she echoed.

"Are you denying that a dead body was found at the lodge today? I was listening to the police scanner. I know what I heard."

"What you heard and what actually happened may not be the same thing. I really don't have time to talk about anything right now, though. My paint is drying out as we speak. It was nice talking to you. Have a lovely day."

She put the receiver down and sighed. "I hope this doesn't drive away our guests."

"Maybe they won't even hear about it," Carl said. "None of them live in Nightshade, after all."

"The papers and news sites in Rochester and Buffalo are sure to cover the story. It may even make some of the Buffalo television channels. We just have to hope that our guests live farther away or that they aren't interested in the news."

"At least the body was in the boathouse, which is quite far away from the main building."

"And it's quite possible that our skeleton died of natural causes," Abigail said. She'd given up on the hope that the skeleton was anything other than real, but the more she thought about it, the more likely it seemed that whoever had died in the boathouse had died of natural causes. Murder was a horrible and unusual event, and she'd already found one murder victim in the past month. Surely, that was her quota for at least a few years.

"My dear girl, I came as soon as I heard the news," the voice in the doorway said. "I can't believe we have another murder to solve."

"Hi, Jessica," Abigail replied flatly.

Chapter Four

"Was it awful?" Jessica asked. "I heard that the body was sitting in one of the boats, his or her skeletal hands still gripping an oar."

"It wasn't anything like that, and I'm not going to talk about it," Abigail replied.

Jessica sighed. "I'm simply trying to help."

Abigail looked at her seventy-five-year-old neighbor and sighed. "The last time you tried to help, you nearly got us both killed."

"Not exactly, but regardless, I did solve the case and help the police put a killer behind bars."

"Yes, well, I'm sure they appreciated your help, but I'm sure they won't need it this time. For a start, it's entirely possible that no one was actually murdered."

"Tell me everything," Jessica said. She crossed to one of the couches in front of the fireplace and sat down. "Come along," she said, patting the seat next to her.

"I need to paint," Abigail replied. "We can talk while I work, if you want, but I really need to get some work done."

She crossed the room to where she'd left her painting supplies and began to unwrap her brush.

Jessica frowned. "Yes, of course. I don't want to interrupt your work."

She got up and walked to the reception desk. There, she grabbed the office chair that was behind the desk and rolled it across the room toward Abigail. Carl stared open-mouthed at her from where he was standing on the other side of the desk.

"Now, tell me everything," Jessica said as she settled herself into the chair.

Trying not to laugh, Abigail opened the paint can and then slowly climbed the ladder.

"Barry came to see me today," she began as she dabbed the brush into the paint.

"Barry Cuda? I'm not certain I would recommend you get involved with Barry Cuda. He has a bit of a reputation, you know."

"Someone suggested that he might be a good person to run a boat rental business for me."

"Someone? Perhaps that someone is less familiar with Mr. Cuda's tendency to drink too much."

"Perhaps."

"Had you arranged an appointment with Mr. Cuda?"

Abigail swallowed a sigh. "I'd called him and left a few messages on his answering machine, asking him to get in touch. He arrived unannounced today."

"Nightshade is a small town. People still like to visit their friends and neighbors without having to make a dozen phone calls first," Jessica told her. "I never call you before I drop in."

I had noticed, Abigail thought. "And this is my business, so he probably assumed that I'd be here whenever he decided to visit."

"And he was correct, of course. Is he going to run the boat rental business for you, then?"

"I've no idea. We haven't even managed to establish the condition of the boats that were left in the boathouse yet. They may need more work than is worth doing, and I may not bother with boat rentals, at least not this year."

"Yes, of course, because when you went down to the boathouse, you found a skeleton inside the building," Jessica said excitedly. "Tell me everything."

"I don't think I'm supposed to tell anyone anything," Abigail countered.

"As your nearest neighbor, I think I'm entitled to know what you found. If there is a killer in the area, I should know about it."

"Whatever happened to the man or woman that we found in the boathouse, it happened years ago."

"But now that the body has been found, the killer must be worried about being discovered."

"I'm surprised the body wasn't found sooner. The killer couldn't have known that Jack and Janet weren't going to use the boathouse for years."

"Unless Jack or Janet did the killing."

Abigail's jaw dropped. "I thought you were friends with Jack and Janet."

"I am friends with Jack and Janet, but I believe anyone can be a killer under the right – or rather, the wrong, circumstances."

"So you're suggesting that Jack or Janet killed the person we found in the boathouse?"

"I'm saying it's one possibility. I'm keeping an open mind for now."

Abigail climbed down the ladder and moved it several feet to the left before climbing back up and going back to work. "Did Jack and Janet know Helena Lane?" she asked as she picked up her brush.

"Helena Lane? Is that who you found? Are you sure? How could you tell?"

"Oh, shoot," Abigail exclaimed. *Of course, Jessica didn't know anything about the coat that Barry thought he'd recognized.*

"You can't leave the story there. Why do you think you found Helena Lane?"

"Barry thought he recognized a coat that was hanging in the boathouse. He thought it was one of Helena's. Apparently, she'd made it herself."

Jessica nodded slowly. "Helena made nearly all of her own clothes. She was very talented. Was the coat green and yellow?"

"I didn't see the coat."

"If Helena's green and yellow coat was in the boathouse, then the skeleton must be Helena. She loved that coat and wore it everywhere."

"It sounds as if you knew her well."

"We both belonged to the Nightshade Sewing Circle," Jessica explained. "Stitches and Notions lets us meet there once a month. We have coffee and cake and talk about our latest projects. If we're stuck on something, we can bring it to the meeting and get help."

"I didn't know there was a sewing circle in Nightshade."

"Do you sew?"

"I don't, but Mandy does. While she's mostly doing set design now, she did some costume design in college. She got quite good with my mother's old sewing machine and eventually bought herself a new model that could do a lot more."

"I have an old machine, but Stitches and Notions has a few machines that they let the circle members use for their projects, so I do most of my sewing in the shop. Helena did all of her sewing there because she didn't have a machine of her own."

"I'll have to tell Mandy to visit Stitches and Notions when she next visits."

"It's a lovely little store with everything you could possibly want for sewing and crafting. I'm sure the owner will remember Helena well."

"Do you remember when you last saw Helena?"

Jessica frowned and then sat back in her seat. After a moment, she pushed one of her feet against the ground, causing the chair to rotate very slowly. After three complete rotations, Jessica stopped and looked up at Abigail.

"I simply don't remember," she said sadly. "She didn't always come to the circle meetings, but she came to most of them while she was living here. At some point, she simply stopped coming, but I can't tell you when that was. I'm sure someone at some meeting commented about it, but I don't remember the conversation. It's been years, though, at least four, maybe five."

"But not as much as ten years ago?"

"Oh, definitely not. And that's an interesting point, now that you mention it. Jack and Janet stopped using the boathouse about ten years ago. As far as I know, they locked it up and no one ever went inside again. If that's right, then the skeleton can't be Helena's. It must be someone who disappeared around ten years ago."

"I'd suspect it was Rusty Morris if he hadn't just turned up dead in the annex," Carl said from where he was still standing near the desk.

"He did disappear about the same time as when Jack and Janet locked up the boathouse. Maybe he had an accomplice of some sort, and maybe Rusty killed the accomplice and hid the body in the boathouse. Maybe that's the real reason why he came back to town last month. Maybe he was planning to get rid of the body before you could find it," Jessica suggested.

"Maybe," Abigail replied.

"I can't see it," Carl said. "We all know who was working with Rusty and where that person is now."

Jessica nodded. "Prison is a good place for murderers. But now I'm trying to remember if anyone else disappeared about the same time as Rusty."

"Bernadette Shaw?" Carl said doubtfully.

"I know where Bernadette went," Jessica told him. "That husband of hers was cheating, and she decided that she wasn't going to put up with it any longer. While she didn't exactly announce that she was leaving, she did tell a few of us where she was going."

"I can't think of anyone else," Carl said after a moment.

"I can't either, and I'm not sure it's worth the time and effort to try. If Helena's jacket was in the boathouse, then it hadn't been locked up for ten years," Jessica replied.

"We don't know that it was Helena's jacket," Abigail pointed out as she moved the ladder again.

"But it was very distinctive. If Barry thought he recognized it, he was probably correct," Jessica said. "Who might have wanted poor Helena dead?" She pushed off again, this time rotating in the opposite direction.

"Barry said she was part of the Nightshade Players," Abigail said.

"Yes, she was," Jessica agreed. "She made some costumes for them for a few of their shows. We all pitched in and helped at one sewing circle meeting, actually. We helped her put together several Renaissance-style dresses for a play that they were doing. It was great fun."

"Do you think someone in the Players killed Helena?" Carl asked Abigail.

"I don't think anyone killed Helena," Abigail replied. "At this point, we don't know who we've found, and we also don't know if the person in the boathouse was murdered or not. It's far too soon to be talking about it like it's a murder investigation."

"The police will probably start with Connie," Jessica said thoughtfully as she stopped the chair.

"Yeah, I would if I were Fred," Carl agreed.

Abigail inhaled slowly. *Don't ask. Don't encourage her.* "Who's Connie?" she blurted out.

"Connie Wallace," Jessica replied as if that answered the question.

"She's Barry's wife," Carl added after a moment.

"Barry's wife?" Abigail echoed. "How long has he been married? He told me that he and Helena lived together for a while."

"They did," Carl agreed. "Barry and Connie have been married for a long time, but they have a sort of, um, well, I don't know what they have, but it isn't a conventional marriage. Connie has a boyfriend, too."

"Interesting," Abigail muttered.

"I forget that you're new to town," Jessica said. "You haven't met anyone yet, have you?"

"I've met a few people, but I've been rather busy here, and I haven't had many opportunities to get out into the community," Abigail replied defensively.

"And not everyone has been kind enough to simply drop in to visit you," Jessica added.

"No," Abigail agreed.

"Barry and Connie have been married for like forty years," Carl said. "She always says that she married him back when he was just Bert Wallace. That was before he joined the Navy. He was only gone for a year or so, but when he came back, he started telling everyone that his name was Barry Cuda."

"Maybe he ran away from the Navy and changed his name so that they couldn't find him," Jessica said darkly.

"Nah, he just thinks Barry Cuda sounds cool," Carl told her. "He got kicked out of the Navy for drinking on duty."

Jessica nodded. "That doesn't surprise me."

"So he and Connie are still married, even though they both see other people?" Abigail asked.

"They bought a duplex right after Barry came back from the Navy," Carl told her. "Barry lives on one side and Connie lives on the other. That way they can both come and go as they please, but they know where to find the other one if they want company. That's how Barry explained it to me, anyway."

Abigail nodded. "So Helena lived with Barry in that duplex?"

"If they lived together, then yeah," Carl said. "I didn't know that they lived together, but Barry's never lived anywhere else, aside from when he was working at the Xanzibar."

"Where did he live when he was working at the Xanzibar?" Abigail asked.

"They had a staff wing," Carl said.

"The main building has several wings," Jessica added. "Most of them are for guests, but one houses the conference facilities, and another was built especially for the staff. Herb wanted everyone who worked there to stay there as well."

"He just wanted everyone to be available twenty-four hours a day, seven days a week," Carl said. "It was a huge hotel, and Herb and Tammy wanted to give guests a five-star experience. They needed a lot of staff in order to accomplish that – staff that didn't mind working all hours of the day and night."

"So Barry lived there, but Connie didn't?" Abigail wondered.

"She had her half of the duplex. She didn't need to live at the Xanzibar. I remember her saying something about staying well away just in case Herb decided to put her to work," Carl replied.

"And when the hotel closed and Barry moved out, he moved back into his half of the duplex," Jessica added. "We all thought, when Barry and Connie bought the property, that they'd rent out half of it, but they never have."

"Do either of you know why Connie has stayed married to Barry for all these years?" Abigail had to ask.

The pair exchanged glances and then Jessica shrugged. "You'd have to ask Connie that question. I wouldn't stay with a man who cheated on me, but Connie doesn't seem to mind. Of course, she's had more than a few boyfriends over the years, too."

"Maybe it's an actor thing," Carl suggested.

Abigail started down the ladder again. "They're both actors?" she asked as she stepped off the bottom rung.

"They're both part of the Nightshade Players," Jessica replied. "I'm not certain that that qualifies either of them as actors."

Carl laughed. "Connie is better than Barry, but then, Barry often has a drink or two before shows, which means he forgets lines now and again. I don't think I've ever seen Connie forget a line."

Jessica sighed. "I like Connie, but she isn't the most expressive when she's on stage."

"She does tend to talk in a monotone," Carl agreed.

Jessica looked at Abigail, who was slowly climbing back up the ladder that she'd just moved.

"She says all of her lines as if she's reading the telephone book," she said. "It's the same way she talks when she's not on stage, and it can be quite disconcerting."

"What do you mean?" Abigail asked.

Jessica shrugged. "It's often difficult to tell if she's telling you good news or bad news. You'll see what I mean when you meet her."

"I doubt I'll ever meet her," Abigail replied.

"She'll be at Helena's memorial service, if nothing else," Jessica told her.

"Everyone in town will be at the memorial service," Carl added.

"Memorial service?" Abigail echoed questioningly.

"Barry will want to have one. If he doesn't, then Neal will insist on it," Carl said.

Jessica nodded and then looked at Abigail. "Of course, you don't know Neal. He's one of the Nightshade Players. I would imagine he thinks he's in charge of the group in some way. He'll want to do something to honor poor Helena, who was such a valued member of the group."

"So valued that no one missed her," Abigail suggested.

"Helena was a very private person who kept to herself," Jessica replied. "She told everyone she met that she never stayed in any one place for long and that she wasn't very good at saying goodbye. After our Sewing Circle meetings, she always used to say that she'd see us next time unless she'd moved on. In the last few months before she disappeared, she started adding that it was likely she'd be gone soon."

"How convenient for her killer," Abigail said softly.

"Indeed," Jessica agreed. "And the more I think about it, the more I suspect that someone from the Nightshade Players killed her."

"Because she got a better part in their next show?" Carl asked, laughing. "Or maybe he or she didn't like the costumes Helena designed."

"As I said before, Helena mostly kept to herself. She did her job, and she did her sewing. I always felt that she belonged to the Sewing Circle only so she could get access to our sewing machines. Nightshade Players was her only other activity," Jessica replied.

"Theater seems an odd choice for someone who kept to herself," Abigail said thoughtfully.

"Not only did it let her pretend to be other people, but the group let her design and make costumes for them. As I said before, she loved to sew and once told me that she'd made enough clothes for herself that she didn't think she'd ever have to shop again. Making costumes gave her an outlet for her desire to keep sewing," Jessica argued.

"And you think someone from the group killed her?" Carl asked.

Jessica shrugged. "It's a working hypothesis."

Carl laughed. "Okay, then. Who? Which one of the men or women in the Nightshade Players killed Helena Lane?"

"That's the question, isn't it? Of course, Fred may have already solved the crime, assuming there was a crime, but if the killer wasn't immediately obvious, Fred may struggle to work out his or her identity. If it is Helena, then whoever killed her has had four or five years to cover his or her tracks," Jessica replied.

"Just how large of a group is the Nightshade Players?" Abigail asked from the top of the ladder.

"It's not huge," Carl replied. "There are only maybe a half dozen members of the group. Obviously, they need more than that for shows, but anyone in town can audition. You don't have to belong to the group if you want to be in their shows."

"So why belong to the group?" Abigail asked.

"Because the group decides which shows to do," Jessica told her. "And they pick the cast as well, after giving themselves the very best parts."

Carl chuckled. "Jessica has been in a few shows over the years."

Jessica flushed. "I think nearly everyone in town has been in a few shows over the years."

"I did one," Carl admitted. "It must have been twenty years ago now. The only thing I remember about it was that I had to kiss Connie Wallace during the show. I suggested that we just pretend, but she wasn't having that. She insisted that we practice until we got it just the way she wanted it." He stared off into space for a minute with a grin on his face. "It was some kiss," he said eventually.

"It was, indeed," a voice said from the doorway.

Abigail sighed. She'd propped the door open to help dissipate the paint fumes, but that meant that people could simply walk in unannounced.

Carl's face turned bright red as the woman, who looked sixty-something, strolled into the room. Her hair was almost the same shade as Carl's cheeks and her eyes were a stunning green that could only be somehow enhanced. Her dress was short and tight around generous curves.

"I don't know that Carl had had much practice with kissing before that show," she said after a moment. "But he definitely had lots of practice after it." She winked at Carl.

"I need to go and, um, tighten something," he said, quickly rushing out of the room before anyone could reply.

"I didn't mean to scare him off," the woman said as she slowly looked around the room. Her eyes didn't seem to miss much before they finally focused on Abigail. "You must be Abigail Clark. I'm Connie Wallace. We really need to talk."

Chapter Five

"Good afternoon, Connie," Jessica said.

Connie looked over at the other woman and nodded slowly. "Jessica," she said flatly.

"We were just talking about Barry," Jessica said.

"I'm sure you were. I suspect everyone in Nightshade is talking about Barry right now. Imagine stumbling across your ex-girlfriend's skeleton in an abandoned building. That sort of thing only happens in books and plays," Connie said.

"Is Barry certain that he found Helena, then?" Jessica asked.

Connie shrugged. "He seemed convinced that it was her when he called me. I don't think the police have confirmed his suspicions, but Barry never lets a little thing like facts get in the way of his drama."

Jessica laughed. "He's a character."

"Yes," Connie agreed with a sigh. "I suggest you choose more wisely than I did if you ever decide to get married," she said to Abigail. "Stay far away from men who are described as being 'a character' in any way."

Abigail smiled down at her from the top of the ladder. "Thanks for the advice."

"You do love him, though," Jessica interjected.

Connie frowned and then nodded slowly. "Of course I love him. We never would have lasted this long if we didn't love each other. We even have fun together, mostly. We just can't stand living together."

"Men do seem to get underfoot a great deal when you have to live with them, don't they?" Jessica asked. "My house felt three or four times larger after my husband passed away."

"What can I do for you?" Abigail asked after a short silence.

Connie looked up at her. "For a start, you can come down and talk to me from the ground. I'm getting a sore neck trying to talk to you up there."

"She's working," Jessica said before Abigail could reply. "There are a number of guests arriving for the weekend, and she needs to have the painting finished before they get here."

Abigail put her brush into the can and then slowly climbed down the ladder. "That's all the cutting in along the ceiling done, anyway," she said as she looked up to check her work. "Now I need to get the roller out and start painting the walls. That should go more quickly, I hope."

"This is the perfect time for a short break, then," Connie replied. "Come and sit down and tell me all about your unpleasant discovery earlier."

"I'm not supposed to talk about it," Abigail told her. "It's a police investigation."

Connie waved a hand. "Barry already told me everything about what you found and why he thinks the skeleton is probably Helena's. I'm not interested in all of that. I want to know how Barry reacted."

"How Barry reacted?" Abigail was confused.

Connie stared at her for a moment and then slowly walked

to one of the couches and sat down. "Please, just give me five minutes of your time."

Stifling a sigh, Abigail put down the paint can and walked over to join Connie on the couch. Before either woman could speak, Jessica quickly wheeled herself over to join them. Connie frowned at her before turning back to Abigail.

"Barry and I have been married for over forty years," she began. "We were both too young to get married, of course, but we didn't think so at the time. We'd only been married for a short while before Barry joined the Navy. He couldn't find a job here, not one that he could keep for long, anyway, so he joined the Navy. Sadly, that didn't work out much better."

"He's always had a problem with alcohol," Jessica said.

Connie nodded. "He has. At least he's a friendly drunk with a fairly low tolerance for alcohol. Once he hits a certain point, usually while he's telling everyone around him how much he loves them, he simply falls asleep."

Jessica nodded. "Wherever he is and whatever he's doing."

"It's quite endearing – for most people. Obviously, employers don't see it that way," Connie said.

"I can understand why," Abigail told her.

"After the Navy, he worked at the Xanzibar for a while. He loved it there, but then they went out of business. He's done a lot of jobs since, most of which only lasted a few months, sometimes even weeks. He's actually more reliable when it comes to shows with the Nightshade Players than he is anywhere else."

"How does he pay his bills?" Abigail asked. As soon as the words left her lips, she blushed. "Sorry, that was a rude question."

Jessica and Connie both laughed.

"Anyone in town could answer that question for you," Jessica said. "Barry's father got hit by a delivery truck from one of the big national delivery companies when he was crossing the main street in town. He sued the company and won a small fortune not long before he passed away. He left the money in trust for Barry. Barry gets a lump sum every month from the trust."

"It isn't a ton of money," Connie said. "But it's enough so that he doesn't have to work if he doesn't want to, as long as he's careful with his spending. And Barry would rather be careful with his money than work."

"He does love the water, though," Jessica said.

Connie nodded. "Sometimes he'll take a job, like the one he took with Scott Wright, just for a chance to spend some time on the lake. While Barry can just about make ends meet with his monthly payments, he can't afford to buy himself a boat, so he's usually happy to work at boat rental places in the summer months or take other odd jobs, if they involve boats or water."

"And he's good at fixing them and keeping them running," Jessica added. "Everyone in Nightshade knows who to call if they have problems with their boats."

"Yeah, he's great," Connie said dully. "But we've wandered off topic. The thing is, Barry and I have an agreement. Maybe I should say that we have several agreements. We share a duplex. Barry has his side and I have mine, but we spend time together, too, sometimes quite a lot of time. Having said that, we also both see other people. That sounds a good deal more exciting than it actually is, though. We agreed that we could see other people twenty-odd years ago. In all that time, I've dated two other men and Barry has only gotten involved with one other woman."

"Helena Lane," Jessica said.

Connie nodded. "The idea of seeing other people is a good deal more exciting than actually getting involved with someone else is."

"I thought you and Ricky were happy together," Jessica said.

"We are, sometimes," Connie sighed. "Relationships are hard work, and being in two at the same time is complicated, that's all. Ricky and I have been dating for a few years now, and once in a while we even talk about maybe getting married one day. Obviously, I'd have to divorce Barry first, but that's just a technicality, mostly."

"Is it?" Jessica asked.

"Yesterday, I would have said yes," Connie said softly. "Today, Barry got himself into trouble, and I was the first person he called. And my first instinct was to drop everything and try to help him. As much as he makes me crazy, I do love him, maybe even more than I'd realized."

"I can't see why he's in any trouble," Abigail said. "It's hardly his fault that we stumbled across a dead body in the boathouse."

"But he and Helena were a couple," Connie replied. "That has to make him the number one suspect in her murder."

"I think you're getting way ahead of yourself there," Abigail told her. "The body hasn't been identified yet, and even if it is Helena, she may not have been murdered. She may have died of natural causes."

"And even if she didn't, the police are probably going to have a hard time proving it was murder," Jessica added. "If she was poisoned or stabbed or maybe even shot, there may not be any evidence left to prove it."

"You're making me feel better already," Connie said. "But I need to know how Barry acted when you were going to the boathouse."

Abigail frowned. "I'm not sure what you mean."

"She means, was he acting like he was nervous because he knew that you were about to find his former lover's body," Jessica explained.

Connie flushed, but didn't speak.

"He wasn't nervous at all," Abigail replied, choosing her words carefully. "In fact, going to the boathouse was his idea. I would have been happy to leave it for another day. I didn't think there was any rush, but he suggested that we needed to see what was down there so that we could start ordering parts to get the boats working again."

Connie sat back and exhaled slowly. "Thank you. I feel much better now."

"You thought Barry killed Helena," Jessica said.

"I did not," Connie snapped. She frowned at Jessica and then looked at Abigail. "I was just worried that Barry might have known something about what had happened to her, that's all. But if going in the boathouse was his idea, then he clearly didn't know what you were going to find."

Abigail nodded. "I'm pretty sure he was just as shocked as I was when we found the skeleton."

"Now we just have to figure out who killed Helena," Jessica said.

Connie stared at her for a moment and then nodded slowly. "That's a very good point, actually. I didn't care for the woman, but she didn't deserve to be murdered."

"I thought she was lovely," Jessica said. "But I didn't know her well," she added.

"She could be lovely, when she was in the mood to be lovely, but she could also be difficult and demanding. I don't think I knew her very well, really, all things considered, but I probably knew her better than most people in Nightshade."

"Of course, Barry knew her best," Jessica said. "Where is Barry? I'd love to hear his thoughts on what happened to Helena."

"As soon as the police were finished questioning him, he went home. He called me while he was walking around the lake along the way. I'm pretty sure he's passed out by now."

"I should get back to the painting," Abigail said, getting to her feet.

"We'll just sit here and talk about the Nightshade Players," Jessica told her. "They have to be at the top of any list of suspects."

Connie frowned. "Those are my friends you're talking about."

"But they were the people in town who knew Helena the best," Jessica countered. "When she used to come to our sewing circle, she used to talk about everyone in the group."

"I can't see anyone in the group being involved in what happened to Helena. We all liked her, and she was a valuable asset to the Players."

"Let's talk about the members," Jessica suggested.

Abigail poured paint into a tray and then checked that the drop cloths hadn't been moved around too much when she'd moved the ladder. She began to work slowly, listening carefully to the conversation behind her.

"There's me and Barry, for a start," Connie said. "And neither of us did anything to hurt Helena. Actually, Barry may have broken her heart a little bit, but that's just because he's an idiot when it comes to women."

"She lived with him for a short while and then moved out," Jessica said. "Why?"

"Why did she live with him or why did she move out?" Connie asked. "She was staying in The Towers, which was very expensive for someone who was waiting tables for a living. She said something about moving in with Barry to save money, but then, after a while, she decided that she wanted to live somewhere a bit nicer than half of a 1960s duplex."

"But she and Barry were still together when she moved out?" Jessica wondered.

"As far as I know, yes. She was still coming to the meetings that the Players had every week. We were just starting to plan for our next show when she left town."

Jessica nodded. "And what was your next show?"

"We were talking about doing a really obscure British play called *Three Gentlewomen from Bologna,* but in the end we decided to go with something a bit better known. That was the year we did two different plays by Forrest Luna. He isn't that well known in the US, but he's huge in Australia, even though he's British. We were right in the middle of Neal's British phase, when he thought he was really good at a British accent and wanted to do nothing but plays that would let him use one."

"I remember that," Jessica said. "I came to see the Agatha Christie play you did, and I remember thinking that it was a good thing I knew the story, because I couldn't understand a thing Neal was saying."

Connie laughed. "It was a bit awful, but it made Neal happy," she said.

"So let's talk about Neal," Jessica said. "I don't really know him well. Tell me about him."

"He's fifty or close to it, but he'll only admit to being past his thirties," Connie told her. "On stage, he's sixty percent ego, thirty percent noise, and ten percent talent. Off stage, he's still mostly ego and noise, but he's usually pleasant – when things are going his way, at least."

"He works for the local bank, doesn't he?"

"Yeah, he's a vice president, a title that feeds his ego even more. I shouldn't say anything bad about him, though, as he was incredibly helpful when I needed to remortgage my half of the duplex."

"Did he get along well with Helena?"

"They were friendly enough. We all get frustrated with Neal sometimes, because he thinks he's in charge of the group. He doesn't like to listen to different opinions, but I can't see him killing Helena because she wanted to try Shakespeare next instead of whatever Neal wanted."

"If Neal had turned up dead, you'd all be suspects," Jessica suggested.

Connie laughed. "That's probably very true. He's a nice person, really, he just likes having everything his own way. I suppose we all do, though, don't we?"

The phone rang, making Abigail jump. She put down the roller and crossed to the desk.

"Hello?"

"Jake Blake. I work for one of the news channels in..."

"No comment," Abigail said firmly before she put the receiver down. She frowned at the device and then turned off the ringer. While she hated the idea of missing calls from potential guests, she didn't want anything to interrupt the conversation the two women were having. If she was going to have the Nightshade Players take part in her Halloween weekend, she needed to know everything she could about the men and women involved. And she was nosy, too.

"Another reporter?" Jessica asked.

"Of course. Sorry for the interruption," she replied.

"We were talking about Neal," Jessica said. "He's not married. Is it possible he was interested in Helena on a personal level?"

"I don't think Neal is interested in that sort of relationship, not with women or men. I've never known him to date anyone."

"Interesting. Maybe he fell madly in love with Helena and killed her because she didn't return his affection."

"I'm pretty sure if Neal killed her, that he had some other motive."

"Such as?" Jessica asked.

Connie shrugged. "Maybe he was afraid that she was going to try to take over the Players. Before she came to town, Neal did most of the work backstage, designing the sets and the costumes and whatnot. Helena was very quick to start taking over some of those jobs. Maybe Neal was tired of her doing things he wanted to do."

"Surely he could have just told her not to do some of them," Abigail suggested.

"Maybe, but we were all happy with Helena's work. Besides, Helena made it clear that she wasn't planning on staying in Nightshade for long. It made sense to take advantage of her talents while they were available."

"But if she was leaving soon, Neal didn't need to kill her," Jessica said thoughtfully.

"So let's move on," Connie suggested. "Maybe Joe had a good reason to kill her."

"Joe? I can't see it. He's a lovely young man."

"Joe?" Abigail asked.

"Joe Cummings," Connie explained. "He's not that young, though. He turned forty-five last year. He's a very talented actor, but he's missing that certain something that makes actors into stars."

"He was also stuck in Nightshade, taking care of his mother for decades," Jessica added.

Connie nodded. "She passed away about six years ago. Joe has been talking ever since about moving to Hollywood to try his luck, but he still hasn't bought a plane ticket."

"He'd be giving up a lot if he went," Jessica pointed out. "He's Scott Wright's IT person," she told Abigail. "I've been told that Scott pays quite well."

"Joe has plenty of money," Connie agreed. "And a nice house and a newish car."

"What about women in his life?" Abigail asked.

Connie laughed. "He has a short attention span. I think he's probably been involved with every single woman in

Nightshade at least twice. He typically dates women from Rochester or Ramsey these days."

"He'll flirt with you when you meet him," Jessica warned her. "Don't fall for his charms, unless you're only looking for something short term."

"I'm not really looking for anything right now."

"Don't tell Joe that," Connie suggested. "He'll see it as a personal challenge."

Abigail made a face. "I hate men like that."

"He's actually very nice," Connie told her. "And he treats his girlfriends well while he's with them. As I said, he just has a short attention span."

"What about him and Helena?" Abigail asked. "Did they get along?"

"As far as I can remember, they were always friendly with one another," Connie replied. "I certainly can't imagine any reason why Joe would want to hurt Helena."

"Who haven't we talked about?" Jessica asked after a moment.

"Ricky, maybe," Connie replied.

"Ricky French is Connie's boyfriend," Jessica told Abigail.

"For the moment, anyway," Connie muttered.

"How long have you been together?" Jessica asked.

"Nearly ten years, two of them happy." Connie laughed. "We make jokes like that all the time. Ricky is nine years younger than me, so I call him my boy toy and he calls me his cougar. I adore him, really, but this thing with Barry has my head all over the place."

"Did he and Helena get along well?" Jessica wondered.

"A little too well sometimes," Connie replied with a scowl. Then she shook her head. "When she first started coming to our meetings, she used to flirt with all of the guys. After a while, she focused her attention on Barry and Ricky. Once she moved in with Barry, she backed off from Ricky a little bit."

Abigail looked over. "Only a little bit?"

"It wasn't a big deal," Connie said.

"Although it does give you a motive for Helena's murder," Jessica said thoughtfully.

Connie sighed. "I knew we'd get to that eventually. Maybe it's time I headed for home. Barry is probably fast asleep, but if he is awake, he may want some company. He was badly shaken by what happened earlier."

"He wasn't the only one," Abigail said.

"Thank you for your time. I appreciate it." Connie got to her feet and slowly walked to the door. "For what it's worth, I didn't kill Helena Lane, or anyone else, for that matter." She walked out of the building before anyone could respond.

Chapter Six

"Well, of course she'd say that," Jessica said after a moment. "But she has to be on the list of suspects."

Abigail shrugged. "We don't even know if Helena was murdered. We don't even know that it is Helena, for that matter."

"Connie ran away as soon as we started talking about Ricky," Jessica said. "That's suspicious."

"Or maybe she doesn't want to consider the man in her life as a potential killer."

"She has two men in her life. Either of them could have killed Helena."

Abigail sighed. "Maybe we should have this conversation after the police work out who they found and whether the person was murdered or not."

"Is that the time?" Jessica asked. "I really must go. I must call Janet and ask her about the boathouse."

"Fred asked me if I have a number for Janet, but I don't. You should call him and give him her number."

"I already have. He caught me when I was on my way

here." Jessica got to her feet and then slowly walked toward the door. "I'll come back to talk again once the body has been identified," she added before she left the room.

"Sure, fine, great," Abigail muttered. She looked at the roller in her hand and then at the half-painted wall in front of her. "I really need to focus on one thing at a time," she said before loading the roller with paint.

"Abigail? Are we having our staff meeting today?" Marcia asked a few hours later.

"It's later than I thought," Abigail replied as she glanced at the clock. "Yes, I'd like to have our meeting as scheduled. I'm actually nearly finished for today."

"I'll let Carl and Arnold know. We weren't sure, with the police here and everything..." Marcia trailed off and then turned and went back toward the kitchen.

Abigail quickly finished the last section of the last wall and then stepped back to see how the room looked.

"You've done a good job," Carl said as he walked into the room.

"It needs a second coat, but I'm happy with it so far. How are the guest rooms coming?" she replied.

"I've finished painting all four guest rooms on the second floor. After the meeting, I'll clear out the mess, and then I'll start on the corridor tomorrow morning."

Abigail nodded. "That's great. I know everything on that floor was painted just a few years ago, but you have to admit that it all looks a lot better now."

"It does. I suspect that we'll need to paint every room at least every other year if we want to keep things looking their best. I've been really careful to cover the carpet in every room. They still look fairly new, at least."

"It sounds as if we're going to be ready for Friday."

"With time to spare, I hope."

Carl helped her clear away the paint and paint supplies while they waited for the others. Marcia arrived as they moved the ladder as far into a corner as possible to get it out of the way. She was carrying a tray that she put down on the desk.

"Coffee and cookies," she explained, gesturing toward the tray.

"You are my favorite person in the entire world," Abigail said as she walked over and picked up a mug of coffee. "I forgot to have lunch and I'm starving." She grabbed a chocolate chip cookie and took a big bite.

"I can make dinner for you a bit early if you want," Marcia offered.

"I don't want to be any bother. A few cookies will keep me going," Abigail replied.

"Sorry I'm late," Arnold said as he rushed into the room. "Fred saw me coming up from my cabin and stopped me to ask me a few questions."

"He had a few questions for me, too," Carl said. "But I couldn't really tell him much."

Abigail frowned as she picked up her notebook. "I have a dozen things to go through with you all. Let's leave what's happening in the boathouse for the end, if you don't mind."

"Sure," Carl replied with a shrug. "You're the boss."

"I suppose I am," Abigail replied with a grin. "And right now I'm more than a little excited about the weekend coming up. Or maybe I should say nervous. That might be more accurate. I've been managing hotels for years, but it all feels very different when it's your own hotel. This will be our first weekend with more than a single guest, and it's our first special event as well. I really want everything to go well."

"It's going to be great," Marcia assured her. "You've

planned everything perfectly, and we're all excited and eager to welcome guests back to the lodge."

"We just have to hope that the police will find out what happened in the boathouse before our guests start to arrive," Carl said.

Abigail sighed. "That might be a bit optimistic. Whatever happened down there, it happened a long time ago. But let's get back to talking about this weekend. Marcia, how are the menus coming?"

"Good, I think. Here's what I'm planning." She handed them each a sheet of paper.

Abigail took another cookie before she started reading. "Mummy meatloaf?"

"You wrap it in bacon and use pearl onions as eyes," Marcia said.

Carl laughed. "Sounds good to me."

"Bat stew?" Arnold asked.

"It's really beef stew, but that didn't sound scary," Marcia replied.

"I think this looks great," Abigail said. "I really appreciate the amount of time and effort you put into all of this. I can't wait to try phantom pancakes for breakfast."

"I'm looking forward to having a chance to make some different things. Jack and Janet were happy with the same meals for breakfast and dinner every week for years and years. I just hope I can remember how to cook other things," Marcia replied.

"We're all excited," Arnold said. "While I shouldn't complain, because Jack and Janet fed me breakfast and dinner every day for all of the years that I've been here, I am looking forward to having something different for a change."

Carl nodded. "But what are phantom pancakes?" he asked.

Marcia laughed. "I've been working on making pancakes

that look a bit like ghosts. I think I've just about got the shape right. I use two small chocolate chips for eyes."

"Maybe we should try some of these things this week," Arnold suggested. "Surely, you'd like some extra practice?"

Marcia laughed. "You just want chocolate chip pancakes."

Arnold nodded. "Absolutely."

"It's up to you," Abigail told Marcia. "You can make whatever you want for meals this week. We don't have guests, so you're just feeding us, and we won't complain. If you want to try out mummy meatloaf every day for the week, that's fine by me."

"I may try a few of the recipes this week if no one minds. And I'll make phantom pancakes for everyone tomorrow."

Carl and Arnold both clapped lightly as Abigail drew a thin line through the word "menus" on her list of things to talk about with the staff.

"Guests arrive on Friday. They'll have dinner, and then we're having a social hour here, in the lobby," she said. "We'll have donuts and warm apple cider for them. Do you think we need an alcoholic beverage as well?"

"The guests won't complain if you do," Arnold said. "I took a class on bartending once, and I still have the recipe books they gave us. Do you want me to look for a cocktail that would be suitable for fall?"

"That sounds good," Abigail replied. "We'll offer one, or maybe two, cocktails for them while they mingle and get to know one another."

"Do any of them already know each other?" Marcia asked.

"If they do, they didn't mention it to me when they reserved their rooms," Abigail replied. "I advertised the weekend on social media, targeting people interested in Halloween and travel. From what I can remember from the reservations, none of the guests live all that near one another, although I believe they are all from New York or Pennsylvania."

"What happens next?" Carl asked. He was taking notes in a small notebook.

"Saturday morning, after phantom pancakes, our guests are welcome to explore Nightshade," she told them. "They're on their own until the afternoon, but the Halloween celebrations will start here around three. We'll have the pumpkin carving contest first. I have six tiny trophies, so everyone will win one. I just have to work out what the different categories should be."

"Scariest, funniest, prettiest, most creative," Arnold rattled off.

"I have all of those," Abigail told him. "But we need two more and I'm stuck."

"Most unusual?" Marcia suggested.

"Best effort?" Carl said.

"Worst effort?" Arnold offered.

They all laughed.

"I'm hoping to get some ideas when I see what everyone has done," Abigail said. "Maybe most modern or most old-fashioned. We'll see what people do with their pumpkins and their tools."

"Tools?" Carl asked.

Abigail nodded. "I bought six sets of pumpkin carving tools from an online shop. They're probably dreadful, but at least everyone will start with the same disadvantage."

"And you have plenty of pumpkins?" Carl checked.

"Not yet, but I will by Saturday. I ordered a dozen, all the same size, from Scott Wright's pumpkin farm. Someone is supposed to deliver them tomorrow."

"What happens after the pumpkins are carved?" Carl asked.

"Apple bobbing and Halloween music, courtesy of DJ GT."

"GT? That's Greg, the state trooper, isn't it?" Carl asked.

Abigail nodded. "I was surprised to learn that he was a DJ in his spare time, but he came very highly recommended."

"He's a great DJ," Arnold told her. "We had him at our wedding, and he's done a lot of other weddings that I've attended."

"I've asked him for a selection of scary, spooky, Halloween-themed songs, with a few more recent popular hits mixed in," she told them. "He's going to start around four and be here until ten, but he'll take a break from six until seven while everyone is having dinner."

"I thought we were going to have a bonfire," Arnold said.

"That's on the maybe list because it's weather dependent. If it's not raining, we can have a bonfire outside. Greg said that he's happy to play music outside, too. He'll be working from a tablet, and he has speakers that are safe to use outdoors."

"So he can move around with the party," Carl said.

Abigail nodded. "I'm still trying to find someone who can tell ghost stories or something similar. Barry suggested that some of the Nightshade Players might be available to dress in costume and wander through, but we never finished that conversation."

"I'm sure they'd add an interesting atmosphere to the party," Marcia said.

"All of the guests are being encouraged to wear costumes," Abigail continued. "And I'd like to encourage you all to wear costumes on Saturday as well."

All three of her staff just stared at Abigail for a full minute.

"Or not," she said eventually.

"I think we're just surprised," Marcia said. "Jack and Janet would never have suggested such a thing."

Jack and Janet don't sound as if they were any fun at all, Abigail thought. "I don't want you to feel as if you have to wear costumes. You do whatever you're comfortable doing. I just thought it might be more fun for everyone if we were all dressed up."

"You're going to be wearing a costume?" Arnold asked.

Abigail felt herself blushing as she nodded. "I love Halloween and dressing up. I have a Wolfram Woman costume from the most recent Xosis Man movie that I thought I might wear."

"I loved her costume," Marcia said. "She looked really evil."

"She did," Abigail agreed. "Evil, but also very comfortable."

Marcia laughed. "Her costume did look a lot more comfortable than most superhero costumes. At least it isn't skintight."

"The skirt is actually shorts with a skirt over the top, and it has pockets," Abigail told her.

"Can we wear the same costume?" Marcia asked.

"I can tell you where I bought it, if you want the same costume," Abigail offered.

"Thank you, but I think I might have the perfect thing already," Marcia said thoughtfully.

"Maybe I could go as Xosis Man," Arnold said. "That wouldn't be a hard costume to make."

"Not at all," Abigail agreed.

"I have an old pirate costume in the back of my closet," Carl said. "It's left over from when I was doing plays with the Nightshade Players. I'm not sure it will still fit, but didn't Xosis Man once fight pirates?"

Arnold laughed. "I remember that movie. The pirates were dressed like Halloween-costumed pirates. It was quite laughable, really. Your old costume would probably be perfect."

"So that's Saturday night," Abigail said. "Maybe you could find another cocktail or two that we could offer that evening," she said to Arnold. "And then make a shopping list for ingredients."

"We could have hot chocolate with peppermint schnapps, too," Marcia suggested. "That's always good around a bonfire. It's supposed to be quite cold on Saturday."

"Cold, but hopefully dry," Abigail agreed. "I can get a bottle of schnapps and some hot chocolate mix." She made a note. "Marcia is going to supply dinner and then snacks for the party."

"It will be finger foods, all themed to Halloween," Marcia told them.

"And no one will notice if you all grab a few snacks during the evening," Abigail told them. "I appreciate that you're all willing to work extra hours over the weekend."

Marcia looked at the others and then shrugged. "Jack and Janet always had us work extra hours when we had weddings or other special events. We're used to it."

"They didn't always warn us in advance, either," Carl added.

"What happens on Sunday, then?" Arnold asked.

"Nothing much," Abigail replied. "Because Marcia is working late on Saturday, we'll be having Sunday brunch instead of breakfast. Guests can get brunch from eleven to one before they check out."

"I'm theming the brunch, too," Marcia said. "One last little bit of Halloween before everyone starts singing Christmas carols."

"We'll talk about Christmas next week," Abigail said with a grin. "And Thanksgiving as well. For now, though, does anyone have any questions about our Halloween weekend?"

"I'm looking forward to it," Arnold said. "I think it will be interesting to do something different. We never had any special events when Jack and Janet were here."

"We had weddings sometimes," Marcia said.

Arnold nodded. "But that isn't the same thing at all."

"I'm glad you're all so willing, and even eager, to help," Abigail said. "Before I met you all, I was worried that some of you might be resistant to change."

Carl grinned at her. "That would be me. But I'm coming around to your ideas, and I know you need to do something to bring in more guests. Jack and Janet didn't care if we weren't busy. They'd paid off their mortgage decades ago."

Abigail looked at her list. "I'm going to be talking to Mandy later today. She did some sketches of how we should decorate the lodge and then went and bought everything we need to accomplish her plans. The box of decorations should be arriving today or tomorrow. As soon as it gets here, Carl and I will need to start decorating."

"I'm going to try to get the corridor done tomorrow," Carl told her. "That will leave me free to decorate on Wednesday and Thursday."

"We should have plenty of time," Abigail replied. "I told Mandy not to get too carried away – not this year, anyway. It's our first attempt at a themed weekend, but it won't be our last. If this weekend goes well, we can build on what we learn for the future."

"I'd feel a lot better about it if the police weren't here," Marcia said, glancing at the windows at the front of the lodge as yet another marked police vehicle rolled past.

Abigail sighed. "We may as well talk about the elephant in the room now. I'm sure you've all heard that Barry Cuda and I found a body — or, rather, a skeleton — when we went down to the boathouse earlier today."

"Was it really on the floor near the door as if it had been trying to get out for years?" Arnold asked.

THE BODY IN THE BOATHOUSE

Abigail stared at him for a moment. "No, not at all. Where did you hear that?"

He shrugged. "There are already all sorts of rumors and stories going around. Nightshade is a small town, and, obviously, the police aren't releasing any information yet. People have overactive imaginations."

"I'm probably not supposed to tell you anything, but I trust you not to repeat what I say. The skeleton was lying in one of the boats. There was a coat hanging on the wall behind the skeleton, and Barry thought he recognized it," Abigail told them.

"That's why people were saying it was Helena Lane," Marcia said. "I couldn't understand why people thought that, since the boathouse has been locked up for over ten years, and Helena has only been gone for five."

"I don't suppose any of you have any idea why Helena might have been in the boathouse?" Abigail asked.

"I can't imagine why anyone would have been in the boathouse, other than Jack or Janet. The door was padlocked shut, wasn't it?" Arnold asked.

"It was, but Barry actually said that he thought the padlock was too new to have been on the door for over ten years," Abigail said. "Jack told me he couldn't find the right key for the padlock, but maybe he never had a key for the padlock that was actually on the door."

"You think someone cut off the padlock that Jack put on the door and then hid the body inside before putting on a new padlock?" Carl asked.

Abigail shrugged. "That's one possible scenario. Did Jack and Janet ever have any trouble with people breaking into the boathouse?"

"Fred asked me that, too," Carl told her. "To the best of my knowledge, no one has ever broken into the boathouse. I suppose I should say that prior to today, I didn't believe that anyone had ever broken into the boathouse."

"I can imagine it happening, though," Arnold said thoughtfully. "And if I had to make a list of people I could see doing it, Barry would be at the very top."

Marcia sighed. "He's a good guy, really, but he does drink a bit too much sometimes, and then he does stupid things."

"Connie said he falls asleep after he's had too much to drink," Abigail said.

"Oh, yeah, he does," Marcia agreed. "But he has a bad habit of doing something stupid first, like letting himself into QuackMart and then falling asleep next to the ice cream freezer."

"I can see him breaking into the boathouse, just so he could be near boats," Arnold said. "He loves boats and water."

"Might he have broken in and taken a boat out for a row around the lake?" Abigail asked.

Arnold and Marcia both shook their heads.

"He's far too smart about water safety to do anything like that," Marcia said. "He doesn't drink when he's around water."

"Maybe he should live on a houseboat," Abigail said.

"Was Barry very upset when you found the body?" Marcia asked. "There was a time when I thought he might actually divorce Connie and marry Helena."

"He was upset, but so was I," Abigail replied.

"I bet he's at the top of the list of suspects, assuming Helena was murdered," Arnold said.

Abigail shrugged. "There seems little point in worrying about suspects at this stage. We don't know who was found, and we don't know what happened to him or her."

"That hasn't stopped Jessica from starting an investigation, though, has it?" Marcia asked. "I swear that woman has spent her entire life training for just such an eventuality."

"What do you mean?" Abigail asked.

"She reads nothing but murder mysteries, and when she isn't reading, she's busy talking to everyone in Nightshade, learning their secrets. She used to be more subtle, but as she's gotten older, she's gotten more direct with her questions," Marcia replied.

Arnold laughed. "She can be a bit nosy, but everyone expects it from her now."

"And she did help solve the last murder," Carl pointed out. "The police might never have solved it without her help."

"I think they would have gotten there in the end," Abigail said. "But I am grateful that it was solved quickly."

"Then you should be grateful that Jessica is on the case," Marcia suggested. "She'll have Helena's killer behind bars before the first of November, mark my words."

Chapter Seven

"Does anyone have any questions or concerns about the weekend?" Abigail asked after a few more minutes of discussion.

"I think it's going to be great fun," Marcia replied. "As long as the police investigation doesn't get in the way."

"At least you can't see the boathouse from the lodge or even from the beach," Carl said. "Our guests might not even realize that anything is wrong."

"Let's hope for that," Arnold said.

"You know you can always come to me with questions," Abigail told them as she got to her feet. "For now, though, I need to call my sister."

"Dinner is at six," Marcia said as she headed for the kitchen with the tray full of dirty dishes. "Baked ham with scalloped potatoes, as usual."

"That's my favorite," Carl replied. "I'll be there."

"You may have a new favorite after this weekend," Arnold said. "I can't wait to try mummy meatloaf."

"That does sound good," Carl agreed.

The two men walked out of the room together, still

talking about food. Abigail's stomach rumbled, reminding her that she'd missed lunch.

"Not long until dinner," she said, patting her tummy. Then she crossed to the desk, sat down, and pulled out her cell phone.

"Hey, Big Sister." Mandy sounded excited when she answered.

"Hey, Little Sister," Abigail replied. "How are you?"

"I'm good. I was just talking to the assistant director, and he told me where he's going next. And then he told me that he's going to suggest to the theater that they hire me to do the sets for the show. It's still off-Broadway, but it's going to be a big show."

"Congratulations. I'm really happy for you."

Mandy sighed. "But I'm supposed to be there. I'm already missing our first Halloween in Nightshade and if I get this job, I'll miss Thanksgiving and Christmas as well."

"But this is what you've always dreamed of doing. Sunset Lodge will still be here if you stop getting jobs or if you decide you want some time off. You have to take these opportunities when you can."

"I knew you'd understand, or at least pretend to understand, but I still feel terrible about not being there."

"I don't mind if you feel a little bit bad," Abigail said with a laugh. "But don't feel terrible. We're doing okay here. Marcia and Carl and Arnold are all hard-working, reliable people. If we get busy, I can always hire someone else as well."

"And I'm doing what I can to help."

"Yes, I know. I found out when I went online to pay the mortgage and discovered that someone had paid the next three months' worth of payments."

Mandy laughed. "I got a bonus. I only used half of it on our mortgage. I kept the other half to use to spoil myself."

"That was some bonus."

"I earned it."

"I'm sure you did."

"Did you get the box yet?"

"I haven't. I'm hoping it will arrive today."

"I can check. Give me a second," Mandy told her. "Ah, it's on the truck for delivery, so it should be there any minute now."

"Great. I can't wait to see what you sent."

"You've seen the sketches."

"I have, and they look amazing. I'm not sure I'll manage to live up to your expectations."

"I'm sure you'll do a great job, but I really wish I could be there. No offense, but I think I have a better eye for setting a stage."

Abigail laughed. "You definitely have a better eye for all things decorative and theatrical. That's why you did the sketches in the first place. If you'd just sent me boxes of decorations, goodness only knows what I would have done with them."

"I'm pretty sure you'd have managed, but I want to help. I want to be there, but if I can't manage that, at least I can feel like I'm a part of our little venture."

Abigail sighed. "There was another complication in our little venture today."

"What sort of complication? Don't tell me you found another dead guest?"

Mandy's tone was teasing, but it still made Abigail flinch. "I found a skeleton."

"Which is perfect for Halloween, isn't it?"

"I found the skeleton of a person in the boathouse."

"A real person? As in someone died in our boathouse?"

"Remember how Jack couldn't find the key to the lock on the boathouse door? Barry reckons that the lock was too new to have been the one that Jack put on the door. It seems likely that someone left the body there and then put a new lock on the door."

"Slow down," Mandy said. "I need to sit down. Okay, now let's start at the beginning. Who is Barry?"

"Barry Cuda is a local fisherman and sailor. Someone suggested to me that he might be a good person to run boat rentals for us this summer. I called and left a few messages on his answering machine, and he finally turned up this morning."

"Barracuda? As in the fish?"

"It's Barry Cuda, C – U – D – A. It isn't his real name, though. Fred, the police detective, said Barry's real name, but I've already forgotten it."

"I think I should be taking notes. Okay, so Barry came to see you this morning. Then what happened?"

"We went down to the boathouse to see if we actually have any boats or not. Barry picked the padlock open and opened the door. He had a flashlight and thanks to that, we could see the boats, and the skeleton that was lying inside one of them."

"Are you sure it was a real skeleton? Maybe, if Barry is so good with locks, he bought a skeleton from a Halloween shop and put it in there as a joke."

"If he had, I'm pretty sure he would have stopped me before I called the police," Abigail replied. "When the police arrived, they seemed pretty sure that the skeleton was real, too."

"So someone hid a dead body in the boathouse," Mandy said after a short pause. "I don't suppose the skeleton was wearing a nametag or had a wallet with identification tucked between its knees."

"I didn't see much of anything besides the boats and the bones. Hopefully the police will find more, but Barry thought he recognized a coat that was hanging on the wall behind the skeleton."

"So he knows who you found?"

"Maybe. Obviously, the police will have to prove it one way or the other."

"I hope this time it won't be someone that I used to date," Mandy said.

Abigail chuckled. "If Barry is correct, it's a woman called Helena Lane. She was active in the local community theater group here, but I don't think you'd have ever had a chance to meet her. I very much doubt that she was ever in a show in New York City."

"Helena Lane?" Mandy echoed. "That doesn't sound familiar."

"I'm just hoping that the police investigation doesn't interfere with our Halloween weekend."

The sisters chatted for a few additional minutes before Mandy ended the call.

"I'm due on set in five minutes. I need to go. Let me know if the box doesn't arrive," she said.

"I will. Love you."

"Love you, too."

Abigail put the phone down and then sighed. The answering machine light was blinking frantically. As she pushed play, she crossed her fingers that none of the calls were cancellations. After deleting seven calls from reporters, she switched the computer on and pulled up the web pages she had designed for the Thanksgiving weekend she'd been planning. Once Halloween was over, she would publish them and then start advertising. What she had to decide next was whether or not to start using more of the guest rooms. Could she and Carl get the rooms on the third floor painted and spruced up enough for guests before Thanksgiving? She was still thinking about Thanksgiving when the delivery truck arrived with the box from Mandy.

"It's a lot bigger than I was expecting," she told the driver after he'd struggled into the lodge with the box.

"I don't know what's in there, but it's heavy," he replied as she signed for the delivery.

Grabbing a pair of scissors, she carefully cut the box open and then looked inside. Mandy had packed everything carefully between layers of paper and packaging, so she couldn't see much. Deciding that doing anything more would simply overwhelm her, she shut the box and pushed it into a corner. Once the painting was finished, she'd tackle the decorating.

"And it's dinner time," she said happily as she looked at the clock. "Everything else can wait until after dinner."

Once her tummy was full of delicious food, Abigail felt a lot better. "Thank you for that," she told Marcia. "I ate too much, and I'm a bit sleepy, but I'm also feeling anxious to get the painting done. I think I'll tackle the second coat in the lobby now instead of leaving it for morning."

"Do you want a hand?" Marcia asked. "I haven't painted anything in years, but I really enjoyed it when I painted my cottage. Let me get the kitchen tidied up and I'll come and paint a wall or something."

"See how you feel after you finish in the kitchen. There's a lot to tidy up."

"This is nothing. Once we start having guests, I'll have a lot to do. Just feeding you and Carl and Arnold isn't even work."

Abigail laughed. "It sounds like work to me. I'd be happy to have some help with the painting, though, if you really want to help. You know where to find me."

Four hours later, before she headed to bed, Abigail stood in the middle of the lobby and slowly turned in a full circle. "It looks a lot better," she said as she studied the results of the hard work they'd done.

"It really does," Marcia agreed. "I can't believe how much difference just a coat of paint made."

"Two coats," Abigail said with a laugh. "I'm really happy with how it turned out, though. It was definitely worth the hard work. I'm going to leave the ladder here because we'll need it tomorrow when we're decorating."

"I'm looking forward to helping with that, too. Jack and Janet used to put a Christmas tree in here, but that was about all they did in terms of decorating for the entire year."

"You all may get tired of putting up and taking down decorations, but I'm looking forward to decorating the lodge for every occasion, including some that I may make up myself."

Marcia laughed. "You're definitely making my job a lot more fun."

"I'm glad to hear that."

Marcia headed back toward the kitchen while Abigail checked that the front door was securely locked. As she headed for the stairs, she wondered if it was time for the lodge to get better security. After two dead bodies in two months, she felt a bit uneasy as she climbed the stairs to the guest room that she was currently using. Once inside, she locked the door and then slid the desk chair across the room, pushing it in front of the door. It wouldn't stop anyone from getting in, but it would make a lot of noise if someone pushed against it. "That will have to do," Abigail muttered as she started getting ready for bed.

"A little to the left," Arnold said. "No, I meant right, or rather I meant your right, my left."

Abigail looked down at him and laughed. "How about here?" she asked.

"That looks wonderful," a voice from the doorway said.

Abigail looked over and smiled at Scott Wright as he walked into the room. The handsome businessman grinned back at her.

"You like our spider?" she asked as she carefully attached the large spider body to the hook she'd just stuck to the ceiling. The spider's eight legs stretched down to the floor below her.

"He's almost cute, actually, if you don't mind spiders," Scott replied.

"I hate them," Abigail replied. "But this one is too big to be real, so I don't mind him all that much."

"Him?" Scott asked, sounding amused.

"His name is Doug, after one of my friends from high school. Doug loved spiders and had a pet tarantula when he was a teenager. He now works in a zoo out west, looking after their spiders and insects."

"I suppose I never thought about zoos having spiders and insects."

"They do, although part of their insect collection is specifically bred to feed some of the animals at the zoo. But what brings you here? Surely you didn't just come to meet Doug?"

Scott laughed. "Had I known Doug was here to meet, I might have done just that, but no, I brought your pumpkin order."

Abigail stared at him for a moment. "You brought my pumpkin order? Since when does Nightshade's richest resident deliver pumpkins?"

"Since I was looking for an excuse to come and see you," Scott replied, his words making Abigail blush.

"Where are the pumpkins, then?" Arnold asked.

"In the back of the truck outside," Scott told him. "Where do you want them?" he asked Abigail.

"Just bring them in here," she suggested. "I'm afraid if we leave them outside they might freeze or get eaten."

"Both real possibilities," Arnold said. "We'll put them along the back wall. No one will even notice them there."

"Some of them are for decorating," Abigail said as she climbed down the ladder. "But most of them are for the carving contest."

"You're really going all out for Halloween," Scott said.

Abigail nodded. "I'm hoping that themed weekends will bring in lots of guests. We don't have that many guests coming this time, but we also don't have all of the rooms ready yet, so it's worked out well. I hope to have more rooms available for our Thanksgiving weekend."

"I want to hear all about your plans after we get the pumpkins inside," Scott said as Arnold walked back into the room carrying two large pumpkins.

"I can help," she offered.

He shook his head. "I think you have your hands full with Doug."

Abigail looked up at the spider and laughed. "I need to get his hands, or rather his legs, into place."

She moved the ladder and then climbed back up, carrying a leg. After carefully sticking it to the ceiling, she went back down for the next one. The eight legs were all arranged across the ceiling by the time the men finished bringing in the pumpkins.

"And now I need a drink," Arnold said as he put down the last large pumpkin. He disappeared, heading for the kitchen, before Abigail could reply.

"Do you need a drink?" she asked Scott.

"I'm fine. I have a mug of coffee in the truck. But how are you? I was shocked when I heard what happened out here yesterday."

Abigail shrugged. "I'm okay. It was unsettling, let's say, but for the moment, it all feels quite unreal. As far as I know, the police still don't know who we found or what happened to him or her."

"According to the local news, Barry Cuda was with you when the skeleton was found."

"He was, yes. I was thinking of having him run our boat rental business this summer. He wanted to see what boats we had and their condition."

Scott nodded. "He's good with boats."

"I feel like there's a but coming."

He shrugged. "He isn't always the easiest person to get along with. He worked for me for a few months, but we didn't agree on, well, much of anything, really. He quit before I could fire him, but only by a few minutes."

"Oh dear. That's worrying."

"Getting rid of him was actually a bad business decision," Scott said after a moment. "I didn't like his attitude or his casual approach to things like working hours and record keeping, but when he was there, he worked hard, and everyone loved him. After he left, I struggled to get anyone to replace him. Eventually, I just gave up and closed the boat rental business. At its best, it was barely profitable, but it did bring more people down to the lake – people who bought dinner or ice cream from my café next door."

"So you're sorry you fired him."

"I'm sorry I couldn't find a way to work with him, which isn't exactly the same thing. Anyway, I just wanted to make sure that you knew what you were getting yourself into with Barry. If you can deal with him turning up late every so often and look past his tendency to keep illegible notes rather than proper records, you'll find him a useful addition to the lodge staff."

Abigail frowned. "I hate when people are late."

"It's been years since Barry worked for me. Maybe he's become more reliable."

"Why do I doubt that?" Abigail asked with a small chuckle. "I'm not sure he's going to want to work for me any longer, anyway. He may want to stay far away from the boathouse."

"Rumor has it that the body, or skeleton, might be Helena Lane."

"Barry thought he recognized her coat in the boathouse. Even if it was her coat, it might not have anything to do with the body, though."

Scott nodded. "The entire town is speculating about what might have happened. I really hope it isn't her. She was a nice person."

"I shouldn't be surprised that you knew her. I sometimes forget how small Nightshade actually is."

"The size is why I make Nightshade my home. I travel a lot, because sometimes Nightshade can feel a bit claustrophobic, but it's home. I'd like to think that I know just about everyone in town. I got to know Helena through the Nightshade Players."

"You belong to the Nightshade Players?"

"You sound shocked," Scott chuckled. "Now I wish I could say that I do, but I don't belong to the group. I do, however, provide them with some financial support for their shows. I met Helena when she and Neal came to see me to see if I'd give them a grant to put together a series of short scenes from Shakespeare. They wanted to do something sort of experimental, and I was happy to agree to help."

"That sounds interesting."

"I think it would have been, but it never actually happened. I'm not sure what went wrong, but the project got canceled and the group did something else instead. I can't remember any of the details now, though."

Abigail frowned. "I hope they don't matter," she said, almost to herself.

Scott stared at her. "You aren't suggesting that a canceled play had anything to do with Helena's death, are you?"

"I've absolutely no idea. We don't even know that it's Helena that's been found. Just ignore me. I've been spending too much time with Jessica."

Scott laughed. "I'm sure she has her own ideas about what happened to Helena. Perhaps you should spend more time with people closer to your age. Are you free for dinner Friday or Saturday?"

"Unfortunately, I'll be working. Our guests arrive on Friday, and Saturday night is the big Halloween party."

"And I'm off to Texas next week. I'm thinking about diversifying a bit and buying a cattle ranch."

"Seriously? Cattle?"

"It will be a good investment if I can find the right person to run the place while I'm not there. We'll see. A Halloween party sounds fun, anyway."

"You're welcome to join us," Abigail said impulsively. "Some of the Nightshade Players are supposed to be coming in costume to tell ghost stories and mingle with the guests. Ideally, if you do come, you should be in costume."

Scott grinned at her. "I haven't worn a Halloween costume in years. Don't be surprised if you don't recognize me when I turn up on Saturday. I'm off to find the perfect costume."

"See you Saturday," Abigail called after him as he rushed out of the room.

Chapter Eight

"I can't believe how wonderful this all looks," Marcia said many hours later as she looked around the lodge's lobby.

"It looks great," Arnold said. "Spooky, but not scary."

"That's what we were hoping for," Abigail replied. She walked to the front door and then shut her eyes. When she turned around, she tried to look at the room as if she'd never seen it before.

Pumpkins and gourds in all colors, shapes, and sizes seemed to be everywhere. Lights shaped like bats twinkled across the mantelpiece and along the front of the reception desk. The huge spider on the ceiling seemed to be staring at her as if contemplating making her his next meal. Cobwebs hung in every corner, and a handful of ghosts appeared to be peeking out at her from hiding places around the room.

"It's good," Carl said.

"Mandy knows what she's doing, even from a distance," Abigail replied. "Now I need to take a million pictures for her."

"Let me get that ladder out of the way first," Arnold suggested.

He grabbed the ladder and then carefully carried it out of the room while Abigail pulled out her phone and began to snap photos. She texted them all to her sister and then sighed.

"I'm exhausted."

"Dinner will be ready in a few minutes," Marcia told her. "I suggest you have an early night after you eat."

"Are we having chicken?" Carl asked.

Marcia nodded. "Same as always on a Tuesday," she replied. "I may start mixing things up a bit after the weekend, though. We'll see how difficult I find making different things. It's been a long time since I made anything other than our standard menu."

An hour later, stuffed full of chicken, rice, and vegetables, Abigail wandered back into the lobby. The man standing behind the reception desk, digging through the papers on it, didn't hear her arrival. Abigail took a few steps backward and then rushed back to the kitchen.

"There's a man in the lobby, going through the papers on the reception desk," she said.

"I'll take care of this," Arnold announced. He got to his feet and stormed out of the room.

Abigail followed the former bodybuilder as quickly as she could.

"What exactly do you think you're doing?" Arnold demanded when he reached the lobby.

The man behind the desk, who appeared to be somewhere near sixty, looked up and shrugged. "No one was here. I thought maybe there was a sign under all of this paperwork giving me a number that I could call for help."

"Like that one?" Abigail asked, pointing to the sign that was on the desk next to the paperwork the man had been searching through.

He glanced at it and then shrugged. "How did I miss that?"

"Please move from behind the desk," Abigail said angrily.

The man put the papers down and then slowly shuffled his way out from behind the desk. "You must be Abigail Clark," he said as he moved closer to her. "I'm Ross Danielson from the *Nightshade News*."

"No comment. Please leave," she replied.

Ross sighed. "New arrivals to Nightshade are always so unwelcoming."

"I'd be a lot friendlier if I hadn't found you going through my papers," she snapped.

"If you want to keep things secret, you should put your papers away," he retorted.

"I would have done just that if I'd known you were going to come snooping."

"Ross, what do you want?" Arnold interrupted.

He looked at Arnold and smiled. "How is your new boss, then? She's been here two months, not even, and she's already found two dead bodies. Does that worry you?"

Arnold laughed. "Not even a little bit. Abigail didn't have anything to do with Rusty Morris's murder, and she'd never even heard of Nightshade when the body in the boathouse got locked in there, whenever that was. As to your first question, my new boss is wonderful. She's doing everything she can to make Sunset Lodge a huge success, and I'm happy I get to be a part of it."

"Can I quote you on that?" Ross asked. "How are you finding Nightshade?" he asked Abigail without waiting for a reply.

"It's a wonderful small town, exactly what I was hoping to find when we bought Sunset Lodge," Abigail replied.

"It appears to be a small town full of secrets, though,"

Ross said. "Two dead bodies in only two months? That seems a lot, doesn't it?"

"I'm not going to talk about the bodies," Abigail told him.

"How well do you know Bertram Wallace?" Ross asked.

"I met him on Monday and talked to him for maybe an hour," she replied.

"And from that short chat, you were prepared to hire him to run your boat rental business? Even though you were well aware that Scott Wright fired the man, presumably because he was often drunk at work?" Ross asked.

Abigail inhaled slowly. "I'm not even going to try to wade through all of that. You made a number of accusations and assumptions, and I'm not answering any of them. I'd like you to leave."

"Jack and Janet always found it useful to stay on my good side," Ross told her. "Everyone in town reads the *Nightshade News.*"

"I'm sorry, but I won't be blackmailed into being polite to you," she replied. "If you want to fill your newspaper with lies or speculation or nasty rumors or whatever else you want to call journalism because I won't answer your questions, you go right ahead and do so. The worst that can happen is that you drive me out of business. I'd rather see that happen than give in to your hinted threats."

Ross looked shocked. "I wasn't hinting at any such thing," he said quickly. "I was just saying that Jack and Janet and I got along well. Nightshade is a small town, and all of the small businesses here try to work together to help one another. That includes the *Nightshade News.* Small town newspapers are dying out everywhere, and the ones that are left are usually owned by some big conglomerate that doesn't really care about the town. They're all about bottom lines, whereas I'm all about doing what's best for Nightshade. That means wanting to learn all that I can about the skeleton that you found in your boathouse."

Abigail sighed. "I'm not sure I'd tell you anything, if I did know something, but I truly don't know anything about the skeleton in the boathouse."

"Nothing?" Ross asked. He frowned as Abigail shook her head. "Tell me about finding Rusty Morris's body, then. Was it horrible?"

"No comment," Abigail replied icily.

"Come on. I'm putting together an in-depth piece on Rusty's murder. Just a few comments from you would really spice it up," Ross argued.

"A man was murdered," Abigail said. "I appreciate that you need to sell papers, but I'm not interested in being a part of your article."

"I could give you a good price on doing some advertising in the issue about the murder when it comes out," he said.

"I suspect that article will do more to hurt my business than help it," she retorted. "And I don't think we have anything further to discuss."

Ross looked as if he wanted to argue, but Arnold took a step toward him.

"Let me get the door for you," Arnold said in a low voice.

"Maybe we could do an interview about the lodge," Ross called over his shoulder as he walked toward the door. "I'd love to hear how you came to buy the place and all about your plans for the future."

"Call me," Abigail suggested. "I'm really busy with our Halloween weekend right now, but if you call me in early November, I may have time to talk to you before Thanksgiving." *And the investigation into the boathouse skeleton should be over by then, too,* she thought.

"I'll call you," Ross agreed as Arnold opened the door for him.

Arnold stood in the doorway for a minute before he pushed it shut. "I'm going to lock this," he said. "I think maybe we should start keeping it locked unless someone is actually behind the desk."

Abigail sighed. "Jack told me that he and Janet left the lodge door open all day, every day, only locking up at night before they went to bed."

Arnold nodded. "But Janet was nearly always behind the desk all day, every day. They even took turns getting dinner, so that there was always someone at the desk."

"We were planning on doing something similar, before Mandy decided to stay in New York," Abigail told him. "I hate the thought of locking the door, but more than that, I hate the thought of Ross Danielson going through my things."

"What was he going through?" Arnold asked.

Abigail crossed to the desk and picked up the papers that were there. "These are just the plans for the decorations," she told him. "Pages and pages of Mandy's sketches for how to decorate the room. I don't think these are what Ross was hoping to find."

Arnold laughed. "I don't know what he was hoping to find, but I'm sure it wasn't that."

"He may have been hoping to find our guest list. Then he could have called our guests and asked them how they feel about staying here now that a skeleton has been found in the boathouse. I'm sure he would have gotten some great quotes, and we would have gotten a lot of cancellations."

"You're probably right. He wasn't lying when he said that he got along well with Jack and Janet, though. He used to publish articles about the lodge a few times each year, talking about its history or about some change they were making here. When they added the annex, they made the front page."

"I'd probably have been a lot nicer to him if he'd been sitting on a couch, waiting to talk to me when I walked out here. I'd definitely have been a lot nicer if he had just come to talk about the lodge and not the skeleton." Abigail sighed. "I was just as unwilling to speak to him last month about the murder. I suppose I should be glad that he didn't actually come out to the lodge then."

"I'm surprised he didn't."

"After tonight, so am I."

The pair chatted for a short while longer, but Abigail soon found herself yawning instead of talking.

"Why don't you head to bed?" Arnold asked as the clock struck nine.

"I usually sit with you until ten," she protested.

"But I officially started work at eight, and I'll probably be here until late tonight," he said with a laugh. "Karen is out with her girlfriends. She won't be home until after midnight. I'll sit here and play on my phone or read until midnight and then forward the phone to my cell and head for home. If I'm lucky, I'll get there around the same time she does."

Abigail started to argue, but a huge yawn cut her off. "Are you sure?" she asked as she slowly got to her feet.

"Good night, boss," Arnold replied.

"Thank you, and good night," she said as she headed for the stairs.

"Witchy waffles for breakfast," Marcia told Abigail the next morning.

"Witchy waffles?"

"I thought the chocolate chips looked a little bit like witches' hats," Marcia told her.

"Enough for our Halloween guests, anyway," Abigail agreed. "No one is going to complain about chocolate-chip waffles even if they look nothing like witches."

"I have warm chocolate sauce to pour over them, if you'd prefer that to maple syrup."

"That's a tough decision. It's a good thing I got some extra sleep last night. Chocolate sauce," Abigail said as Marcia put a plate with a large steaming waffle on it down in front of her. "No, maple syrup. No, chocolate sauce." Abigail sighed. "It's a tough decision," she said apologetically.

Marcia nodded and then walked back into the kitchen. When she came back, she was carrying a plate of bacon and two small syrup pitchers. "I brought you both. You need to try them both so that you can tell our guests how they taste, anyway."

Abigail laughed. "Thank you for finding a way for me to avoid having to make a decision." She cut up her waffle and then poured syrup on one half and chocolate sauce on the other.

"Good morning," Carl said as he joined them.

"Witchy waffles with chocolate sauce or maple syrup," Marica told him.

"Or?" he repeated. "Why not and?"

Marcia and Abigail both laughed.

Half an hour later, Abigail walked into the lobby and smiled at Arnold. "Get the chocolate sauce," she told him. "It's delicious on the witchy waffles."

"Better than maple syrup?" he asked.

"I thought so. Carl thought a bit of both was better, but I found that too sweet."

"I never had to make these kinds of decisions when Jack and Janet were here," Arnold said as he got to his feet. "And that isn't a complaint," he added with a wink.

Abigail sat down behind the desk and looked at the notes that Arnold had left her from overnight. Things had been quiet, with only a few calls from reporters from nearby Buffalo calling to ask about the skeleton, and two wrong numbers. She crumpled up the notes and tossed them in the wastebasket at her feet.

"Back to work on the Thanksgiving weekend," she muttered as she fired up the computer.

Two hours later, she was more or less satisfied with what she'd put together. The next step would be to talk everything through with the staff. There was no point in advertising a special Thanksgiving feast if Marcia didn't want to cook it, and she'd need help from Carl and Arnold to get everything else to come together. As she sat back in her seat, she remembered that she'd never made any actual arrangements with Barry for the Halloween weekend. The Nightshade Players weren't an absolutely necessary part of the Halloween party, but she wanted to include them if she could.

"Hello?"

"I hope I didn't wake you," Abigail said when the phone was answered.

"No, no, ah, heck, yeah, you did," Barry replied. "Ever since Monday, I've been drinking too much and sleeping too late. I probably shouldn't tell you that, though, should I? You'll never give me a job if you think I'm an old drunk fool."

Abigail hesitated and then decided to ignore most of what he'd said. "I was just calling to see if you'd had a chance to talk to the rest of the Nightshade Players about the Halloween party on Saturday."

"Ah, yeah, that, I mean, I mentioned it to a few people, but we never actually, that is, I'm not sure what we said. I'm going to have to call you back."

"I'd appreciate it if you'd call back today. If the Nightshade Players can't do it, I'm going to have to find someone else who can."

"We'll do it," Barry said, his voice confident. "I mean, I will, anyway. I can tell a few ghost stories and look spooky all

THE BODY IN THE BOATHOUSE

by myself. But I'm going to try to get a few of the others involved, too. I'll call you back before six."

Abigail winced as the phone clattered loudly as Barry hung up.

"What's next?" she asked herself as she put the phone down.

A loud knocking noise made her jump.

"Someone is at the door," Carl said as he walked into the room.

Abigail nodded. "I realize that. I forgot to unlock it when I came in after breakfast."

"We should probably keep it locked anyway. That will stop people like Ross Danielson just walking in unannounced." Carl crossed to the door and opened it.

"Have you heard the news?" Jessica asked as she rushed into the room. "It's all over the *Nightshade News* website."

"What news?" Abigail replied.

Jessica sighed. "I would have thought you'd be taking more of an interest in local news, really."

"I am interested, but I'm also busy," Abigail told her. She turned back to the computer on the desk and reached for the mouse.

"Never mind that, I'll tell you everything," Jessica said as she walked over to the desk.

Carl followed her, clearly trying to look as if he wasn't hanging onto the older woman's every word.

"What's happened, then?" Abigail asked.

"They've identified the body," Jessica replied.

"That was quick," Carl said.

Jessica nodded. "Apparently, Helena had to have some dental work done while she was living here. When Dr. Stout heard that the skeleton might be hers, he went to the police with his x-rays."

"So it was Helena Lane," Abigail said.

"It was. According to my source with the police, it was also definitely murder," Jessica replied.

"How can they possibly be sure?" Carl asked.

Jessica shrugged. "My source wouldn't tell me any of the details, but apparently the case is now a murder investigation."

"Poor Helena," Abigail said softly. "And poor Barry. I just talked to him. He didn't say anything about the skeleton."

"I heard he's been drowning his sorrows since he found it in the first place," Jessica told her. "He knew it was her as soon as he saw her coat. The question is, did he know she was there before you even got there?"

"If he knew she was there, why would he have suggested that we go and look around the boathouse?" Abigail asked.

"Maybe he forgot about her. Maybe he killed her in a drunken rage and then blacked out. Maybe he only remembered what had happened when he saw the skeleton," Jessica suggested.

"Or maybe he had nothing to do with Helena's death," Abigail replied.

"Someone killed her," Jessica said.

"Assuming your source is correct, at least," Carl muttered.

Jessica frowned. "Regardless of what happened to her, there's going to be a memorial celebration for her tomorrow."

"Tomorrow? Someone arranged that very quickly," Abigail said.

"I was told that Barry made all of the arrangements yesterday, just in case it turned out to be Helena. What he told Scott Wright was that he wanted to have a memorial for her, whether the body is hers or not," Jessica replied.

"That doesn't even make sense," Carl protested.

"Yes, well, I gather Barry was drunk and upset when he called Scott," Jessica explained. "I got all of this secondhand through someone who overheard part of the conversation, but apparently Barry kept talking about how much he'd loved

Helena and how heartbroken he'd been when she left. He told Scott that he wanted to do something to celebrate her life, and that if the body wasn't hers, at least he could celebrate the wonderful woman he'd loved and lost."

"Am I the only one who thinks that odd?" Abigail asked.

"Everyone in Nightshade thinks it's odd," Jessica told her. "And we all think it makes it more likely that Barry killed Helena, too. I'm sure this has moved him to the very top of Fred's list of suspects."

Abigail sighed. "And Barry is supposed to be attending the Halloween party here on Saturday night."

Jessica frowned. "I do hope I'm invited. Perhaps I'll get an opportunity to confront Barry about the murder."

Chapter Nine

"No one is confronting anyone about anything at the Halloween party," Abigail said firmly. "We're going to have a number of guests here, and I'd rather they didn't know anything about the skeleton in the boathouse. You are welcome at the party, but only if you promise not to talk about the skeleton."

"And it's a Halloween party? Am I supposed to come in costume?" Jessica asked.

"I expect most people will come in costume, but it's up to you," Abigail told her.

"Oh, if I can come in costume, then I definitely will. It's been years since I've been to a Halloween party. I wonder if any of my old costumes will still fit," she replied.

"The party starts around seven," Abigail told her.

Jessica nodded. "But, of course, I'll see you tomorrow at the memorial celebration. It's at the Lakeside Restaurant, which is why Barry was talking to Scott. It starts at three o'clock tomorrow afternoon. Apparently Barry wants people who remember Helena to share their memories, and then there are going to be some light hors d'oeuvres and drinks."

"Wow, Barry put that together really quickly," Abigail said.

"Knowing Barry, there will be lots of drinks," Carl said. "But it will be a cash bar."

Jessica nodded. "I was surprised to hear that he's paying for hors d'oeuvres, to be honest."

"He must have loved her a lot," Carl said. "Connie won't be happy."

"I wonder if she'll be there," Abigail said.

Carl and Jessica both looked at her.

"She'll be there," Carl said.

"Everyone in town will be there," Jessica added.

After Jessica left, Abigail and Carl walked through the entire lodge, making sure that everything was ready for their guests who would be arriving in a few days.

"I told everyone that they could check in any time after three," she told Carl as they inspected the guest rooms. "I don't know if any of them will arrive that early, though."

"The rooms are ready, all except for the one you're using," he replied. "It doesn't really matter when the guests arrive."

"We need to check the annex rooms, too. I suppose I may as well move back out there tonight. I can get the room I've been using in here ready now, then."

They checked over the rooms they were planning to use in the annex. After lunch, Abigail packed her bags and moved them into one of the spare annex rooms. With that job done, she got the last of the second-floor rooms ready for their guests. By the time she'd made the bed and then washed all the used bedding and towels, it was nearly time for dinner.

"Can I help in any way?" she asked Marcia as she wandered into the kitchen.

"Everything is just about ready," Marcia replied. "But what's this I hear about a memorial service tomorrow?"

"I believe Jessica described it as a memorial celebration,

rather than a service. It's at three o'clock at the Lakeside Restaurant."

"Barry probably isn't allowed in any of the local churches," Marcia said. "I'm surprised Scott is letting him have it at the Lakeside, though. I didn't think he and Barry got along very well."

Abigail shrugged. "I've no idea."

After another delicious dinner, Abigail spent some time brainstorming ideas for their Thanksgiving and Christmas getaway packages. She was searching the internet for Christmas cookie recipes when Arnold walked into the lobby just after eight o'clock.

"Good evening," he said brightly. "I'm late."

She laughed. "We should probably talk about your hours, actually. You shouldn't work twelve hours a day, seven days a week."

"You know I don't work anything like that much," he countered. "I'm here until ten most nights and then back at six for two more hours. That's four hours a day, seven days a week, which isn't even a full-time job."

"Except you're on call for all the hours in between."

"Let's not worry about that for now. When we start having guests every night for weeks or months on end, we can talk about my hours. At the moment, I'm not even sure why you're paying me to sit here every night and every morning. The phone rarely rings, and no one ever comes to the door."

"I'm not paying you," she reminded him. As part of the sales agreement when Abigail and her sister bought the property, Jack and Janet had agreed to pay the staff through the end of the year. They'd made the offer in an effort to get the sisters to agree to the purchase right away, and it had worked.

He nodded. "We're all expecting you to renegotiate everything to do with our jobs once you are paying our salaries," he told her.

"I'm going to sit down with each of you, probably in December, to talk about your jobs," Abigail replied. "I want to do everything I can to make sure that you all stay."

Arnold laughed. "I can't see any of us leaving unless you fired us. We all love Sunset Lodge. At one point, we were talking about pooling all of our money and buying it ourselves, but then we all agreed that actually running the place was too much work."

"It's a lot of work, but I wouldn't say too much," Abigail said, yawning over the words.

"It seems to be exhausting," Arnold teased.

They chatted for a while longer before Abigail headed out to the annex. When she'd dumped her suitcases there earlier, she hadn't bothered to unpack anything, something she regretted now that she was tired from the long day. It took her half an hour to unpack before she fell into bed.

"What do I wear to a memorial celebration?" Abigail asked Marcia over breakfast the next morning.

"Dark gray would be better than black," Marcia told her. "Brown or dark blue would also work. No white. No bright colors. Having said all of that, goodness only knows what Barry will be wearing. And he may want everyone in hot pink if that was Helena's favorite color."

Abigail sighed. "I was hoping this was going to be easy."

"I'll call a friend and find out," Marcia promised.

An hour later, as Abigail went back through the guest list, second-guessing the rooms she'd assigned to each couple, Marcia joined her.

"Barry is asking everyone to wear bright colors, especially red and pink," she told Abigail. "He doesn't want it to feel like a sad occasion."

"Red and pink? I'll have to see what I can find," Abigail replied.

Abigail, Marcia, Arnold, and Carl had decided to go to the memorial celebration together in Abigail's car. Carl gave her directions to the Lakeside Restaurant from the passenger seat.

"It's lovely here," Abigail said as she parked in the large parking lot. The restaurant was right on the edge of the lake, which gave the building incredible views.

"The parking lot is going to be full soon," Marcia remarked as they walked together toward the entrance.

Abigail looked at the line of cars that was waiting to turn into the parking lot and swallowed a sigh. It really did seem as if everyone in town had come to the celebration, and she couldn't help but feel as if most people would be staring at her. She was probably the only person in town who'd found two dead bodies in the past two months, after all.

The door led into a large entryway. They were quickly shown into a spacious banquet room. Chairs had been arranged in rows in front of a platform that held a single row of chairs with a small lectern in front of them. There were clusters of people scattered around the room, and, from what Abigail could see, nearly everyone was wearing bright colors. She couldn't see a single person in black or even gray.

"Things will be starting soon," the woman who'd met them at the door said before she headed back to the entrance.

"What now?" Abigail whispered.

"Now we find Barry and pay our respects," Marcia told her. "He'll be over by the bar, I'm sure."

The large bar ran along one side of the room. Four bartenders were busy taking orders. Abigail didn't recognize anyone as she followed Marcia across the room. They found Barry leaning against the bar. He had a drink in one hand and an unlit cigar in the other.

"Barry, I'm sorry for your loss," Marcia said.

"Ha," Connie muttered from where she was standing next to her husband.

Barry glanced at her before he looked back at Marcia. "Thank you," he said. "Helena's death is a sad loss for everyone in Nightshade."

"Of course it is," Marcia agreed.

"Excuse me, Mr. Cuda, but I need a moment of your time," a man said.

The man in the dark suit frowned as Barry swayed slightly before he nodded. Connie sighed and then took Barry's arm and led him across the room after the other man.

"There you are," Jessica said as she reached them. "We need to talk to the men and women from the Nightshade Players. I feel as if they're the most likely suspects, don't you?"

"I don't know, and I don't intend to get involved in a police investigation," Abigail replied.

"Yes, of course, but you did want to talk to them about your Halloween party, didn't you? I do hope you aren't trusting Barry to make all of the arrangements," Jessica replied.

Abigail looked over at Barry, who was doing his best to catch the attention of one of the bartenders. She sighed. "It would probably be a good idea for me to speak to some of the other people involved in the group," she admitted. "About the Halloween party, not the murder," she added quickly.

"Yes, of course," Jessica said with a satisfied smile.

"Ladies and gentlemen, we're about ready to begin. If everyone could please take seats, we'll get started," the man who'd wanted to talk to Barry said loudly.

A few people headed for the bar, clearly eager to get drinks before they sat down. Everyone else began to move slowly toward the rows of chairs.

"There they are," Jessica hissed in Abigail's ear. "Let's sit behind them."

Jessica took her arm and pulled her across the room.

Arnold, Marcia, and Carl rushed to keep up with them. As they slid into seats, Jessica leaned forward and tapped one of the men in the row in front of them on the shoulder. He appeared to be in his fifties, with dark black hair that was clearly dyed.

The man turned around and smiled brightly at Jessica. "Mrs. Fleming, how lovely to see you here," he said. "I mean, obviously the circumstances are incredibly sad, but it's always lovely to see you."

Jessica nodded. "It's nice to see you, too, Neal. Have you met Abigail Clark yet? She's the new owner of Sunset Lodge."

Abigail smiled and gave the man a small wave.

"It's a pleasure to meet you," the man replied. "I really must speak with you, actually. Barry said something about you needing a few actors for a party on Saturday?" He made the statement sound like a question.

Abigail nodded. "We can talk after the service."

"Excellent," the man replied before he turned back around in his seat.

Jessica sat back and sighed. "I do hope this won't take too long," she said quietly.

Up on the small platform, Barry and the man in the suit appeared to be disagreeing about something. Barry kept shaking his head while the other man simply kept talking. Eventually, Barry held up a hand.

"She was my girlfriend," he said loudly. "We're going to do things my way."

Before the other man could react, Barry turned and faced the crowd.

"Good afternoon," he said. "It's nice to see you all here. We're here to commemorate the life of Helena Lane. Helena was a wonderful woman who was cruelly and suddenly taken away from us. I could talk about her all day, but before I say anything, I want to invite everyone who knew her to come up and say a few words about Helena."

An awkward silence followed Barry's words. Abigail could see a few people around the room whispering to each other. There seemed to be an almost collective sigh of relief when Jessica stood up and started to walk toward the front of the room.

"During the short time she was here, Helena joined the Nightshade Sewing Circle. She was an incredibly talented seamstress who made many of her own clothes. She was also a kind and caring woman, and I will miss her," Jessica said when she reached the lectern.

As she made her way back to her chair, a man near the back of the room stood up and walked forward.

"That's Peter from the Nightshade Diner," Jessica whispered to Abigail. "Helena worked for him."

Peter looked nervous when he faced the crowd. "Helena was one of the best waitresses I ever had the fortune to work with," he said. "She was very popular with the customers and with everyone at the diner, too. I've been missing her since she left."

He jumped off the platform and rushed back to his seat as two other people stood up. One had formerly lived in the apartment next door to Helena's and the other had worked with her. They both said much the same thing about what a wonderful person Helena had been. As the second person finished speaking, the man in front of Jessica stood up.

"Neal Ford, but you already knew that," Jessica whispered.

Abigail nodded and then studied the man as he walked to the front of the room. He seemed to be taking his time, almost as if he were dragging his feet. The entire thing felt almost theatrical to Abigail.

When he reached the lectern, he turned around slowly and

then stared out at the crowd. Inhaling deeply, he let out a long sigh.

"What can I say?" he began, his deep voice projecting across the room. "I'm devastated." He shut his eyes and took several slow breaths.

Someone in the back of the room coughed loudly.

Neal's eyes flew open, and he frowned. "Devastated," he repeated. "Helena was, well, first and foremost, she was alive."

A few people giggled.

"By that I mean she was full of energy and enthusiasm for life," Neal continued. "She came to Nightshade seeking new experiences. Her entire life had been about seeking new experiences. We, at the Nightshade Players, were incredibly fortunate that she decided to grace us with her many talents. As you've already heard, her sewing skills were significant, and our little troupe never looked better than they did in the shows where Helena took charge of our costumes."

"As if you let her take charge," someone in front of Abigail muttered.

Abigail looked at Jessica. "Joe Cummings," Jessica mouthed.

Joe looked to be somewhere around forty-five. He had light brown hair that had clearly been carefully styled to look slightly tousled. Abigail thought he looked like the sort of B-list actor who got killed first in every bad movie ever made.

Neal looked out at everyone. "It's incredibly difficult for me to think of that amazing woman that I knew no longer being with us. Oh, I was able to accept that she'd left Nightshade. She was never going to stay here forever. No, Helena was too much of a free spirit to stay in one place for long. I realized that the first time that I met her, and I treasured every single interaction that we had because I was always conscious that she wasn't going to remain in our family for long."

"Thanks," Barry said from behind Neal.

Neal looked back at him and then turned back to the crowd. "I knew she wasn't going to stay forever, but I fully expected her to leave Nightshade and go on to do other amazing things. I hoped that she might share some of those adventures with us, either through postcards or email or telephone calls. When those things never materialized, I simply assumed that she was too busy experiencing life. Of course, I never once imagined that anything horrible might have happened to her."

"Of course not," Joe muttered.

"It is simply too horrific to consider that poor Helena was murdered," Neal said. "How could anyone have chosen to harm the wonderful, vibrant, brilliant, and amazing woman who was Helena Lane?" He stopped and then turned his head and very slowly looked around the room, seemingly inspecting the crowd, almost as if he was looking for someone.

"Thank you very much," the man in the suit said. He'd been standing next to Barry, but he took a step toward Neal.

Neal nodded but didn't move away from the lectern. "Someone murdered Helena," he said in a solemn voice. "If that someone is here, and let's face it, everyone in town is here, that someone should step forward now and admit his or her guilt. Whoever you are, you've had five years of living in freedom after having committed the most heinous of crimes. You robbed the world of one of its brightest lights. Come forward now. Admit your transgression. Pay your debt to society."

A long and increasingly awkward silence followed Neal's words. Eventually, Barry stepped up to the lectern.

"Is there anyone else who would like to speak?" he asked, not looking at Neal.

Abigail heard a few people muttering under their breath, but no one stood up.

"Thanks," Barry said to Neal.

He stood and stared at the man until Neal finally nodded and then slowly walked back to his seat. As soon as Neal was seated, Barry spoke again.

"If no one else has anything to say, I suppose I should say a few words. I don't know what to say, though, except that I cared very deeply for Helena and I'm devastated by her death."

He paused and then took a deep breath. "I can't say anything more. Please stay and have a drink or two and talk about Helena for a while. It's what she would have wanted," he said eventually.

The man on the platform with Barry looked as if he wanted to add something, but as soon as Barry finished speaking, people were on their feet, heading toward the bar and the tables of food. Jessica stood up slowly.

"Now, my dear," Neal said as he stood up and turned around to face Abigail. "How many of us did you need for your little party?"

Abigail looked at Marcia and then back at Neal. "Barry suggested that some of you could dress up and mingle with the guests," she explained. "And I was hoping that maybe someone could tell ghost stories."

"I know a number of ghost stories," Joe said.

"Ah, Ms. Clark, this is Joe Cummings, our young star," Neal said, his tone almost mocking.

"It's a pleasure to meet you," Abigail told Joe.

"Likewise," he replied.

"I think we can all manage a few ghost stories," another voice said.

"Of course, of course," Neal said, nodding at the man who'd been sitting on his other side. "This is Ricky French," he told Abigail. "Another of our star performers."

Ricky, who looked no more than fifty, had brown hair and sparkling green eyes. He laughed. "I'm never going to be a star, but I don't mind. I have fun on stage, and off stage as well."

"I'd be delighted if all three of you could come to the party on Saturday," Abigail said. She paused and then flushed. "I don't know if you would expect to be paid for such things?"

Neal shook his head. "While we are professional performers in our hearts, we're an amateur theater group. When we perform shows, we sell tickets to help cover our expenses, but none of us ever gets paid for his or her time or dedication. We do what we do because we love performing. For events such as your Halloween gathering, we would attend simply for the joy of taking part. We also love supporting our local community, of course, and helping your little business to succeed is part of that."

"He means we won't charge you anything," Joe interjected. "I'm happy to come, whatever the others are doing."

"I'll be there," Ricky said. "And I'll bring Connie with me. We'll do costumes that work together. It will be fun."

"I hope so," Abigail said.

"But what do you all think happened to Helena?" Jessica asked.

"I'm sorry I'm late," said a loud voice that managed to cut through all of the noise.

Abigail turned and stared at the woman in the doorway. She was dressed all in black, from the veiled hat on her head to the black shoes that were just peeping out from under her floor length skirt. A quiet murmur went through the crowd. Abigail looked at Jessica, who just shrugged.

"I did so want to be here to hear what you all had to say about my mother," the woman added with a small smile.

Chapter Ten

Several people gasped. Abigail looked over at Barry, who was still standing near the raised platform. He looked stunned.

"I'm Melody, by the way," the woman continued. "Melody Driver. I suppose I should be grateful that the good people of Nightshade were willing to come together to celebrate my mother's life. I'd appreciate an opportunity to speak to each and every person here who knew my mother. I'm going to try hard to forget, for the next hour or so anyway, that someone in Nightshade murdered her."

Melody strolled farther into the room as another wave of surprised noises filled the space. No one else spoke as Melody stopped to talk to a small group clustered near the door. At least ten minutes ticked past before the room slowly began to return to normal.

"She had a daughter," Jessica said in a low voice. "She certainly never mentioned her when we talked."

"I was completely unaware of her existence," Neal said. "And we once had a long conversation about children." He looked at Abigail. "I always imagined that I'd have children

THE BODY IN THE BOATHOUSE

one day, but sadly, I never found the right woman with whom to have them."

Abigail nodded. "And what did Helena say about children?"

"She was sympathetic to my situation, but now that I think back, I don't recall her saying anything about her own circumstances. At the time, I assumed that she also had never had children, but now I think she may have simply talked around the subject, without ever saying anything one way or the other," Neal replied.

"She could be very evasive," Joe said. "It sounds terrible when I put it that way, but I don't know how else to say it. We used to talk at rehearsals, sometimes for hours, and afterwards I'd realize that I'd told her a million things about me and learned nothing about her in return."

Ricky nodded. "I never really thought about it at the time, but you're right. She was very good at getting you to talk about yourself, and also very good at never answering any questions about herself. As surprised as I was to see her daughter walk into the room, now that she's here, I wouldn't be surprised if another half dozen children turned up."

Jessica sighed. "I thought Helena and I were friends. I told her so much about my children. I can't believe she never even mentioned that she had at least one of her own."

"Unless this Melody woman isn't who she claims to be," Neal said in a dramatic whisper. "Maybe she's an imposter. Maybe she's hoping to get her hands on Helena's money."

"Did Helena have any money?" Abigail asked.

"I don't think so," Joe said. "She worked at the local diner. I'm sure she did well with tips, because everyone said she was very good at her job, but even so, she wasn't ever going to get rich working there."

"So maybe Melody isn't after money. Maybe she's after something else," Neal said. "What could she want?"

"Maybe she's a police plant," Ricky suggested. "Maybe they think the killer will be overcome with remorse when they meet Melody and suddenly confess to everything."

"I can't see Fred doing anything like that," Jessica said. "I don't think the police are allowed to make up stories to try to get confessions, anyway."

"Well, I don't trust her," Neal said, staring hard at Melody who was slowly making her way around the room, talking to each group of people in turn. "I intend to be polite, but nothing more, when she gets to us."

"I think that's all any of us can do," Joe replied.

"Did you know that Helena had a daughter?" Neal demanded as Barry and Connie joined them.

Barry shook his head. "We talked about kids. I told her that Connie and I had wanted some when we were first married, but that they'd never arrived. She, well, really she talked around the subject without actually saying whether she had kids or not." He sighed. "She did that a lot."

"Exactly," Neal exclaimed. "I said that exact same thing. When we talked, I felt as if she said she'd never had children, but when I think back, she never actually said any such thing. She was evasive."

Barry nodded. "Evasive is a good word."

"I thought so," Neal replied smugly.

Abigail looked over and saw that Melody was getting closer. *Why are you getting nervous?* she asked herself. *You didn't even know the dead woman.*

"Good afternoon," Melody said as she joined them a moment later.

A few people muttered replies while Neal loudly cleared his throat.

"On behalf of the Nightshade Players, a small amateur group of dedicated theatrical professionals, of which your mother was a very welcome and valuable member during her short time in Nightshade, let me be the first to offer our most sincere condolences on your tragic loss," he said in a rush.

Melody raised an eyebrow. "You're the Nightshade Players? Mom talked about you guys a lot."

"She did?" Neal asked, clearly surprised.

Melody chuckled. "We spoke almost every day, but I'm going to guess that she never mentioned me to any of you."

"She did not," Neal replied.

"Mom didn't like to talk about herself," Melody explained. "She found other people fascinating, but she thought her own life was fairly dull, and she preferred to keep things to herself."

"I can't believe she never told me she had a daughter," Barry said softly.

"She wasn't ashamed of me," Melody said quickly. "But she knew if she told people about me that there would be questions. She didn't like to answer questions – not about her private life, anyway."

Neal nodded. "We were just saying that she was evasive."

"I suppose that's one way to put it," Melody said, her tone suggesting that she wasn't happy with that particular word.

"She was a very special woman with a real talent for sewing," Neal said after an awkward silence.

"Yes, when I was a child, she used to make all of our clothes. Of course, being a typical child, I didn't appreciate the time and effort that went into what she did. I wanted to go to the mall and buy my clothes like everyone else," Melody replied with a sigh. "I'd love to go back now and tell my mother how much I appreciated her hard work. She made everything I'm wearing today."

"That skirt is beautiful," Jessica said. "From a distance, it looked quite simple, but up close, I can see how much effort went into it."

Melody nodded. "And it has pockets," she said with a grin.

"All clothes should have pockets," Abigail said.

"I'm Ricky, um, Ricky French. I was in a few shows with your mother while she was here," Ricky said after another long silence.

"It's nice to meet you," Melody replied. "I remember Mom talking about you. She said you were very talented and that if you ever left Nightshade you could become a star."

Ricky blushed bright red. "Ah, thanks," he said, looking at the ground.

"I'm Connie Wallace, Ricky's girlfriend," Connie said, sliding an arm around Ricky as she frowned at Melody.

"I remember Mom talking about you, too," Melody replied. "She said you were incredibly kind to her, even though she'd started seeing your husband."

Connie flushed and then chuckled. "Yeah, well, Barry and I have an agreement."

"At one point, Mom thought you two might finally get divorced, but then she told me that you'd decided to get back together. I guess that didn't work out," Melody said.

Connie looked surprised. She glanced over at Barry and then slowly shook her head. "Your mother must have misunderstood something that someone said. Barry and I haven't talked about getting back together for more than fifteen years."

Melody frowned. "I'm sure my mother said..." she trailed off and then sighed. "I suppose it doesn't much matter now, does it?" she asked.

"No, I suppose not," Connie agreed.

"I'm Joe Cummings," Joe said, jumping in as Connie took a step backward. "It's nice to meet you. Your mother made me the most amazing costume for one of our shows. I still have it. It's one of my favorite things."

"Thank you," Melody said. "I'm so happy to hear that

people have things that bring back fond memories of my mother."

"She was a very special and talented woman," Neal said.

Melody nodded. "I miss her every day."

"You must be relieved to finally know what happened to her," Jessica suggested.

Melody looked at her for a moment before nodding slowly. "It's been very difficult, not knowing. I should have reported her missing, of course, but I never once suspected..." She trailed off again.

"But I haven't introduced myself," Jessica said. "I'm Jessica Fleming. I used to sew with your mother with the Nightshade Sewing Circle."

"It's a real pleasure to meet you," Melody replied. "My mother talked about the sewing circle and how fortunate she felt to have access to good quality sewing machines on a regular basis. Sewing fed her creativity and made her feel alive."

Jessica nodded. "She told me the same thing. But if you spoke to her nearly every day, why didn't you file a missing person report?" she asked.

Abigail winced at the abruptness of the question. Melody just shrugged.

"Mom was a free spirit and a wanderer. She never stayed in one place for long and she never liked to feel as if she had to stay in touch, either. I'm a grown adult and quite capable of looking after myself. I've been on my own since I was eighteen, and for many years Mom didn't call me at all."

"How sad," Jessica exclaimed.

Melody shook her head. "She wanted me to learn to survive on my own. I'd been difficult to live with during my high school years." She laughed. "More than difficult, actually. I'd been impossible. I thought I knew everything. I hated her for making me change schools every year or so because she'd decided it was time to move again. The day I turned eighteen, I moved in with my boyfriend and told her that I never wanted to see her again."

"Oh my," Jessica said.

"I was an idiot, of course, and totally unprepared for the real world, but my boyfriend and I learned a lot very quickly, and eventually, I reached out to Mom to apologize. It took me nearly six months to find her. It had been six years since we'd talked, and she'd moved seven times in those years, but I finally tracked her down and we started over again, getting to know one another as friends," Melody explained.

"Did you stay in touch after that?" Jessica asked.

Melody nodded. "More or less. Sometimes we'd talk daily for six months or more, and then sometimes we'd go a month or two without speaking." She shook her head. "I let Mom take the lead, really, letting her call me most of the time. Of course, that wasn't entirely my fault. She got a new phone every time she moved to a new area, so I rarely had a working number for her. She kept moving, too, every six to twelve months."

"And then she came to Nightshade," Jessica said. "And you spoke regularly?"

"Not at first. She called me from Nightshade after she'd been here for a few weeks. We hadn't spoken in three or four months at that point. But she really liked Nightshade. The first time she called me, she told me that she thought she might have found the place she'd been looking for her entire life."

"Nightshade is a very special place," Neal said.

"I've only been here for a very short time, but it already feels very special," Melody replied. "Of course, it's difficult for me to forget that my mother was murdered here."

"Had she ever said anything similar about anywhere else?" Jessica demanded.

"Not to me. Usually, when she called me from somewhere new, she would give me a quick rundown of the pros and cons of the place. We'd lived in dozens of towns and cities during my childhood, and, of course, she'd lived many other places after that, so she'd often compare her new temporary home to somewhere else that she'd been in the past. She'd tell me that the new town was about the same size as this place, or smaller than that place, or had a strip plaza that was very similar to the one we'd shopped at in wherever. She didn't do any of that for Nightshade."

"Interesting," Connie said.

"Of course, she also talked a lot about Barry. Is he here?" Melody asked, glancing around the room.

"That's me," Barry said, stepping forward. "I'm Barry Cuda."

Melody smiled at him. "My mother rarely got romantically involved with anyone. She preferred life on her own. I was surprised when she told me that she was going to move in with you, and even more surprised that you stayed together for something like six months."

Barry nodded, his eyes on the ground. "I loved her," he said quietly.

"And I believe that she loved you, in her way," Melody replied. "I don't know that she would have ever married you and agreed to stay in Nightshade, but I know that she cared about you more than anyone else she'd met in her life."

"Really?" Barry looked up, his face red and his eyes filled with tears. "I really did love her."

Melody nodded. "She knew that."

"But she moved out of his place," Connie said. "We all thought she was leaving town. Or rather, we all thought she did leave town."

"I'm not sure what happened," Melody replied. "I need to talk to the police, to tell them what I do know, though. It isn't much, but I'm really hoping it will be enough to help them work out what happened to my mother."

"When did you last speak to her?" Jessica asked.

Abigail swallowed a sigh. *It's a good thing Fred isn't here. He'd never allow Jessica to keep asking so many questions,* she thought.

Melody shrugged. "It was late May or early June, I think. We'd been talking nearly every day, but I'd been out of town, visiting a friend, so I'd missed a few of her calls. I called her when I got home and we had a short chat, but she was on her way out to meet someone for dinner. She told me that she'd call me again in a few days, but not to worry if it was longer, because she was thinking of taking a trip of her own. I asked her if she was leaving Nightshade, and she said that she wasn't sure what she was doing. Now that I think about it, I should have pushed her for more information, but at the time I just assumed she'd tell me more the next time we spoke."

"Of course, you couldn't possibly know that it mattered at the time," Connie said soothingly as Melody wiped away a tear.

"Was it unusual for her to be uncertain as to her plans?" Jessica asked.

"Very unusual," Melody replied. "When she decided that she was ready to move on, she usually packed and left within forty-eight hours. I hated that when I was a child because I never had much time to say goodbye to my friends, but it suited Mom."

"You don't know where she was planning on going?" Jessica asked.

"She said she was thinking of taking a trip, which was different, too. She didn't usually leave a town or city until she was ready to move to the next one." Melody sighed. "At the time it didn't seem important."

"When did you start to worry?" Connie asked.

Abigail sighed. *Anyone else have a rude question for the poor woman?* she wondered.

"She'd told me not to worry if I didn't hear from her for a while," Melody replied. "So I didn't worry for a few weeks or even a month or so. Then I tried calling her cell phone, but the number had been disconnected. I assumed that meant that she'd moved on again, so I just waited for her to call me."

"And five years flew past," Neal suggested.

Melody nodded. "She'd often talked about living off the grid, moving somewhere where cell phones didn't work and living off the land for a while. When I didn't hear from her for months, I assumed that she'd done just that. I figured she'd get back in touch once she'd tired of that lifestyle."

"You couldn't have known," Connie said, patting Melody's arm.

"Good afternoon," a voice said from the doorway. "I'm looking for Melody Driver."

"Who is that?" Melody asked.

"The police," Neal replied in his most dramatic voice.

Melody sighed. "Good afternoon," she said as she walked toward Fred. "I was hoping to meet everyone before I had to talk to you."

Fred shrugged. "I just found out that you were in town. I'd like to speak with you rather urgently."

Melody stopped next to him and then turned and looked around the room. "I'm not sure where I'm going to be staying, but I'm hoping to remain in Nightshade for several days. If I didn't get to meet you this afternoon and you have memories of my mother that you'd like to share, I do hope you'll find time to track me down to share them."

The room was silent as Melody and Fred left the room.

"That was just plain fascinating," Jessica said as the door shut behind the pair.

"It was," Neal agreed. "I'm still not convinced that she's who she claims to be."

"I think we should go," Abigail said to Marcia.

Arnold and Carl, who'd been standing silently next to Marcia since the service had finished, both nodded emphatically.

"I'm ready," Marcia said.

"Call me," Neal told Abigail, handing her a business card. "We'll finalize the arrangements for Saturday."

"Thank you," she replied, slipping the card into her purse.

The foursome headed for the door. It appeared that everyone had had the same idea, as the room was rapidly emptying.

"That wasn't at all what I was expecting," Marcia said as Abigail drove them back to the lodge.

"Me either," Abigail agreed.

"Everyone seemed surprised that Helena had a daughter," Arnold said.

When they arrived back at the lodge, Abigail sat down behind the desk and deleted a bunch of messages from the answering machine. With that out of the way, she went back to work on her plans for Thanksgiving and Christmas. It was nearly time for dinner when someone knocked on the door.

"Ah, good afternoon," Melody Driver said brightly when Abigail opened the door. "I do hope you can help me. I need a place to stay for a few nights."

Chapter Eleven

After everything that had been said at the memorial service, Abigail wasn't terribly surprised, but she wasn't thrilled, either.

"We have a group of people arriving for a special Halloween-themed weekend tomorrow," she told Melody. "I can find you a room, but I'm afraid you're going to find yourself in the middle of all of that."

"Oh, I love Halloween," Melody replied. "I even have a costume in my suitcase."

Abigail was momentarily speechless. "Okay, great, well, um, come in and let me see what I can do," she said eventually. Back at the desk, she opened the computer and looked at the list of available rooms. She was really stalling for time, because she knew exactly what was available.

The entire lodge was empty at the moment, and they weren't using every room for the Halloween weekend, but that didn't mean she had empty rooms that she thought were appropriate for guests.

"I'm afraid all I have available are rooms in the annex," she told Melody after a minute.

"I'm happy anywhere. I just need to be in Nightshade for a while. I need to meet everyone who knew my mother. I need to find some sort of peace here."

"I'll put you in 4A. Let me find the key. Do you want one key or two?"

"One is fine. I usually travel on my own."

Abigail opened the safe behind the desk and then opened the small box that held the room keys. It took her only a moment to dig out one of the keys for the correct room.

"How long do you think you'll be staying?"

"At least through the weekend."

Abigail put her credit card through. "I'll show you to your room, then."

"Oh, you don't have to do that. I'm sure I can find it."

"I don't mind. I was looking for an excuse to stretch my legs." *And if you're going to complain about the room, I'd rather get it out of the way sooner than later,* she thought.

Abigail led Melody back out the front door and then around the building to the small annex behind it. As they went, she explained about the meals that would be available and about the party on Saturday evening.

"The Nightshade Players are supposed to be coming in costume to add some atmosphere. They're going to tell ghost stories as well."

"Are they? Wonderful. I'm looking forward to getting to know them better. My mother told me so much about all of them."

Abigail opened the door to 4A and then stepped back. "Here we are," she said.

Melody walked into the room, dragging her suitcase. She stopped just inside the door and turned around and smiled at Abigail. "It's exactly what I need. It's small, but it's clean and comfortable. My mother and I often stayed in places that were neither of those things."

"It sounds as if you had an interesting childhood."

Melody laughed. "It was definitely interesting. Unfortunately, I didn't see it that way at the time. Looking back, I should have appreciated it more, but while I was living it, I longed to just stay in one place. I wanted my mother to buy a house, so I could paint my walls and put up pictures or posters. We always rented, of course, and sometimes stayed in motels for days or weeks on end while my mother looked for a new job in a strange city."

"I can't imagine."

"I wish now that I was more like my mother. She loved the adventure of it all. Every new city or town brought new sights and sounds and people. I wish now that I'd felt that excitement. Instead, I dreaded meeting new people and going to a new school." Melody sighed. "I know it's pointless, wanting to change the past, but I can't help but have regrets for so many things."

"I'm sorry," Abigail said, not sure how else to respond.

"Mostly, I'm sorry that I didn't report her missing five years ago. I just kept thinking she'd get back in touch eventually. The five years went past very quickly, too. Time gets away from you when you're busy. And I'm always busy. I use work to keep me from thinking too much."

"What do you do?"

Melody laughed. "I'm a real estate agent. After a childhood filled with constant moves, I now help people find their dream homes. In some ways, I think I'm trying to rewrite my own history every time I help someone else find a home, but then I tell myself that I'm overanalyzing things. I do that a lot, actually. I've been in and out of therapy a dozen times, and I suspect I'll be doing more once I've actually started to believe that Mom is truly dead."

"I'm very sorry for your loss."

"Thank you. And thank you for coming to the memorial

service today. I don't believe you'd ever met my mother?" Melody made the statement a question.

"No, but everyone else from the lodge had met her, and I felt as if I should be there."

"And you found her, didn't you? You and Barry? That's what I was told, anyway."

Abigail nodded slowly. "We did, yes."

"Where is the boathouse?"

I was hoping you weren't going to ask that, Abigail thought. "If you follow the path to the lake, you'll see the path to the boathouse on the left. I'm not exactly sure where they've put the police tape, though. You may not be able to get very close."

"I'm not sure I want to get very close. I haven't decided yet if I even want to see it. I was mostly asking so that I don't stumble across it by accident."

"It's out of the way, down a long and overgrown path."

"I am going to want to walk down to the lake, though. I find water soothing. Is there a path around the lake?"

"Not all the way around, but nearly. If you turn right when you reach the water, you can walk about three-quarters of the way around. You have to follow the road to cover the last bit, which includes the section where the boathouse is located."

"So the path to the boathouse doesn't connect to the path around the lake?"

"It does not. You can only reach the boathouse by that one path. Or by boat, I suppose."

"Good to know. Thank you."

"Dinner should be ready now, if you're hungry. Of course, you can eat any time before seven."

Melody looked at her watch and then shrugged. "I'm not very hungry. I may just take a short walk and then have an early night. I don't expect to sleep, but I need to try."

"If you need anything, there's a member of staff on call all night," Abigail told her.

"Thank you."

Abigail went back into the lodge and headed straight for the dining room. Arnold and Carl were already at the table. Marcia walked in as Abigail arrived.

"We have a guest," Abigail told them. "Melody is going to be staying with us through the weekend."

"Melody? Helena's daughter?" Arnold asked. "I did wonder, when she said at the memorial thing that she was going to be staying in town for a few days, if she was going to turn up here."

"Well, she has. I've put her in 4A, in one of the rooms that we had ready for the guests arriving tomorrow. We'll need to get another room ready before they start checking in," Abigail replied.

"Did you warn her about the Halloween party?" Marcia asked.

"I did warn her, and she told me that she loves Halloween and had a costume in her suitcase."

There was a moment of stunned silence before Marcia spoke again.

"Good for her. I'm sure Helena wouldn't want her sitting around feeling sad," she said.

Carl nodded. "I only met Helena once or twice, but Marcia is right."

"Yeah," Arnold agreed. "Helena was a character. My wife did a show with the Nightshade Players during the time Helena was doing the costumes. Karen thought the world of her."

"That's good to hear," a voice said from the doorway. Melody walked into the room. "I decided I should try to eat."

"Absolutely," Marcia said. "Let me get you some dinner.

And everyone else, for that matter." She laughed as she rushed out of the room.

"Tea or coffee?" Arnold asked, walking over to the table in the corner.

Melody frowned. "I don't drink either after noon. It keeps me awake, which is probably not even relevant tonight, as I don't think I'll sleep anyway, but I'd rather have water or a nice glass of wine."

"We don't serve alcohol at Sunset Lodge except on special occasions," Abigail said, trying not to sound apologetic about the policy that she had no intention of trying to change.

"Water is fine, then," Melody replied.

Arnold nodded and then disappeared into the kitchen. When he returned with Melody's water, Marcia was right behind him. She put plates full of food in front of Carl and Melody and then dashed back to the kitchen. Just a few seconds later, she delivered plates for Abigail and Arnold.

"So what do you think of Nightshade so far?" Arnold asked Melody as everyone started eating.

"It's a lovely little town," Melody replied. "I can see why my mother was so enamored by it. Everyone has been friendly and welcoming and kind and if I didn't have a life waiting for me back in Pittsburgh, I might be tempted to stay for a lot longer than just a few days."

"Pittsburgh is a great city, but it's a big city. Nightshade is very different," Arnold said.

Melody nodded. "I live in the suburbs, of course. I'm not a big city person." She sighed. "I've been there for a long time, nearly all of my adult life, and I've been thinking about moving elsewhere, but every time I think about it, I freeze. I promised myself, when I moved to Pittsburgh, that I was never going to move again."

"You are allowed to change your mind," Marcia said.

"Is it awful that I think I only stayed there as long as I have because I wanted to prove something to my mother?" Melody asked. "My therapist is going to have a lot to say when I get home."

"Abigail said you're coming to the Halloween party," Carl said after an awkward silence.

Melody nodded. "I love Halloween. It's probably another relic of my childhood, but when you're always the new kid in school, it's wonderful to have a chance to dress up and pretend to be someone else, at least once a year."

"Who or what are you going to be for the party?" Arnold asked.

"I have a standard witch costume that gets dragged out most Halloweens," she replied. "My mother made it for me many years ago. Oh, my," she said, as tears began to slide down her cheeks. "I wasn't expecting that to set me off."

"I'm sorry," Arnold said quickly.

"The weather has been mild for October," Marcia interjected.

Everyone worked hard to keep the conversation light for the rest of the uncomfortable meal.

"Thank you. Everything was delicious," Melody said as she scraped up the last of the chocolate icing on her plate. "Very delicious," she added after she'd eaten that last bite.

"You're very welcome," Marcia told her. "I'm glad you enjoyed it."

"So, what is there to do for fun in Nightshade?" Melody asked as she got to her feet. "I'm going to guess that you don't have a lot of wild nightlife."

Carl laughed. "We don't have any wild nightlife. For a few short years, back when the Xanzibar was open, we had something approaching nightlife, but they didn't really encourage the locals to come and drink and party there, or so I've been told. It closed before I was old enough to drink – legally, anyway."

"The bar at the Lakeside Restaurant is nice," Marcia told Melody. "I wouldn't recommend any of the other bars downtown, though. Most of them aren't very female friendly."

"Maybe they just haven't met the right female yet," Melody said with a laugh. "I think I may have to go barhopping and see what I can find."

She sailed out of the room before anyone could reply.

"Is she going to be okay?" Abigail asked.

"She'll be fine," Arnold assured her. "The bars aren't dangerous, just unfriendly to strangers. Most of them are full of men who are drinking to get away from their wives. At worst, Melody will be ignored."

"She'll probably get her fair share of inappropriate comments," Marcia added. "But she seems as if she can handle herself."

Abigail nodded, but she wasn't happy. "I'm going to go and have a quick chat with Melody," she told Carl as the pair walked back to the lobby. "I'll lock the front door so that no one can walk in while I'm gone."

He shrugged. "I can sit at reception if you want to leave the door unlocked. Not that I expect anyone to come in, of course, but I don't have anything else to do."

"But you're supposed to be finished with work today."

"I was just going to go to my cottage and read a book. I can do that here and save you the trouble of locking and unlocking the door." He sat down behind the desk and pulled a book out of one of the drawers.

"What are you reading?" she asked.

"M.D. Cooper's latest release," he told her. "It's science fiction."

Abigail looked at the spaceship blasting across the cover and shrugged. "Not my genre, but it looks interesting."

"M.D. has over a hundred books in the same world and I'm planning to read them all."

"Good for you." Abigail left him to his reading and headed for the annex. When she reached 4A, she hesitated. *It isn't really my place to interfere in the personal lives of my guests,* she thought. *But if anything terrible happens, I'll feel guilty forever.* She sighed and then knocked.

When Melody opened the door a moment later it was obvious that she'd been crying.

"You seemed upset over dinner," Abigail said awkwardly. "I just wanted to make sure you are okay."

"Thank you. That means a lot to me. Not many people care about me," Melody replied, tears streaming down her cheeks. "My mom was all that I had, really, and now she's gone."

Melody burst into tears and threw herself into Abigail's arms.

"I'm so sorry," Abigail said soothingly, patting the woman's back. "It's going to be okay."

After several minutes, Melody lifted her head. "Excuse me," she said, disappearing into the room. Abigail made a face as she listened to Melody loudly blowing her nose. It was several minutes before she rejoined Abigail at the door.

"I should have invited you inside," she said. "I'm just not myself."

"That's understandable. Like I said, I wanted to check on you. I'm not sure you should be going out drinking."

Melody shrugged. "I think I need a drink or two. Or maybe ten. I know alcohol isn't the answer to all my problems, but it might be all that gets me through the night."

"Do you want some company?" Abigail surprised both of them by asking.

"I would love some company. I'll be ready in ten minutes." Melody shut the door in Abigail's face before she could reply.

"You are a complete and utter idiot," Abigail muttered as she walked back toward the lodge. "What were you thinking?

You weren't thinking, obviously. You need to do more thinking."

"I'm sorry?" Carl looked up from his book.

"Sorry. I was just talking to myself. I'm going to have to lock the door. I'm going to go out with Melody for a short while."

Carl stared at her for a moment. "I can stay until Arnold comes on duty," he said. "Call me if you need me."

"I won't be drinking. I'm going to drive."

"Like I said, call me if you need me."

Abigail swallowed a sigh. "Thanks," she muttered as she turned back around. If she was going out, she should probably at least brush her hair.

Ten minutes later, she walked out of her room at the same time as Melody walked out of hers.

"Let's go," Melody said excitedly. She turned and began a brisk walk toward the lodge, her short skirt swishing as she power-walked in six-inch stilettos.

"I'm underdressed," Abigail grumbled as she rushed to keep up.

Melody stopped in the middle of the parking lot. "Maybe we should take a taxi."

"I'll drive. I don't mind not drinking."

"But it will be so much more fun if we both drink. Let's get a taxi. I'll pay for it."

Abigail shook her head. "I'd rather drive. I can't drink anyway. We have a guest staying with us."

Melody slowly turned her head back and forth as if scanning the parking lot. "I don't see any guests, or rather, I don't see any guests who will mind if you get a bit drunk with a friend."

"Thank you, but there are state laws to do with managing a hotel," Abigail replied, making things up as she went along.

"I can't be incapacitated in any way while we have guests staying on the property."

"Well, that's no fun."

"It does save you taxi fare."

Melody smiled brightly. "More money for drinks."

"Whatever," Abigail said under her breath. "My car is over here."

She led Melody to her small SUV and unlocked the doors. They climbed inside and Abigail started the engine.

"I think the Lakeside is our best bet," she said as she pulled out of the parking lot.

"We can start there. I assume that every bar in town is within easy walking distance of the Lakeside."

"I'm not actually sure. I've never looked for bars."

"Then this will be a useful exercise for you. You really ought to know what's available for your guests."

Abigail nodded. As much as she hated to admit it, Melody was right. She should know what bars were available in Nightshade.

A few minutes later, she parked in the small parking lot next to the Lakeside Restaurant. The bar was right inside the door.

"It's dark and elegant and I hate it," Melody said loudly as they walked into the room.

"Good evening," the man behind the bar said as they approached. "You are welcome to find a table or sit at the bar. We have a menu of bar snacks available."

"We don't need food. We just need drinks," Melody told him. "I'll have a whiskey sour."

"Just water," Abigail said.

"This place is overpriced," Melody announced as, drinks in hand, Abigail led her to a corner table.

"What shall we talk about?" Abigail asked as Melody slid into her chair and took a large swallow from her drink.

"We can talk about why they charge so much for their drinks," Melody suggested. "And why they are so stingy when they pour, too."

Abigail took a sip of her water and slowly counted to ten. By the time she reached nine, Melody had finished her drink.

"Let's go find somewhere with a bit more atmosphere," Melody said. "And cheaper drinks," she added, glancing at the bartender.

Melody was halfway across the room before Abigail managed to get to her feet. By the time Abigail reached the door, Melody was strolling along the sidewalk, looking intently at each building as she passed them.

"This one," Melody announced in front of The Hemlock.

Abigail looked doubtfully at the rundown old building. A few neon signs advertising beer flickered in the windows. "Co d B r" and "Op n" flashed on and off as Abigail tried to think of a reason to leave. Melody pulled open the door and a burst of eighties music hit Abigail's ears.

"Perfect," Melody said. "I know every word to this song." She was singing loudly off-key as she disappeared into the bar.

Sighing, Abigail rushed after her. Before her eyes had adjusted to the light, she heard someone calling her name. Turning around, she spotted Barry waving from a crowded booth in the corner.

"Perfect," Melody said as she gestured toward Barry. "I've been wanting to talk to the Nightshade Players."

Chapter Twelve

Melody strolled across the room. When she reached the booth in the corner, she grabbed a chair from a nearby table and pulled it up to the table's end. Abigail followed, stopping to stand awkwardly behind Melody.

"Hey," she said. "It's great to see you all. I assume you're here, mourning for my mother."

"Yeah," Barry said after an uncomfortable silence.

"Sorry for your loss," someone muttered.

"Everyone slide over and make room for Abby," Barry said.

Ricky and Connie both squeezed in closer to Barry, leaving about eight inches of space on the edge of the seat for Abigail. Deciding that was better than standing or arguing, Abigail perched on the seat and hoped that Melody would get bored with this location as quickly as she had the previous one.

"Can I get you something?" the waitress asked, cracking her gum.

"Whiskey sour, a large one," Melody replied.

"Water," Abigail said.

The waitress stared at her for a moment before shrugging and walking away.

"This is nice," Melody said. "The bar is crap, but I'm excited about the company. I was hoping to have a chance to talk to all of you."

"We were just talking about going up to the lodge tomorrow for a chat," Connie said.

"Really?" Melody asked. "But Abigail has a whole bunch of guests arriving tomorrow. This is better."

A few people exchanged glances, but no one replied. The uneasy silence was broken by the waitress.

"One large whiskey sour," she said. "And a water." She handed Abigail a large bottle of water. Abigail knew from the fancy label that she'd made an expensive choice. The bottle's top was half-open, which meant she couldn't send it back and just get tap water.

"Put those on my tab," Barry said before either woman could pay.

"I was going to get them," Neal said.

"Put those on Neal's tab," Barry said happily.

Neal frowned. "You offered first."

"But it means more to you," Barry said.

"Helena was your girlfriend. I would have thought that you'd want to buy her daughter a drink or two," Neal argued.

Connie laughed. "You know Barry better than that. He's never wanted to buy anyone a drink in his life. He's never wanted to buy anyone anything in his life."

"That isn't fair," Barry protested. "I've bought you plenty over the years."

Connie raised an eyebrow. "Plenty of what?"

As everyone laughed, Melody took a sip of her drink. "So, tell me about my mother," she said after a moment. "What did she like about Nightshade?"

"Barry, mostly," Joe said.

This time, as everyone in the group laughed, Melody seemed to be studying them closely.

"What was she like when she was living here?" she asked as the laughter died out.

"She was friendly and fun to spend time with," Connie said. "She seemed really interested in people and their stories. She really took the time to get to know everyone in the group."

"You can say that again," Neal muttered.

"She was a very talented costume maker," Joe said. "We never looked as good, before or since, than we did the year that she made our costumes."

"She made me a gorgeous dress," Connie added. "I still have it and love it."

"And she never mentioned me? Not to any of you?" Melody asked.

"She never talked about her own life," Barry said. "We used to talk for hours about everything, but now that I look back, we talked about nothing. Nothing significant, anyway."

Melody nodded. "What shows did you do when she was here?"

Abigail sat back and listened as the group told Melody all about the three shows they'd done while Helena had been in town.

"And then we were going to do something completely different," Neal said. "We hadn't decided exactly what, but we were planning to do something that would really showcase your mother's talents. Sadly, she left town before we had an opportunity to do that."

"Except she didn't leave town," Melody pointed out.

Neal sighed. "It's so very difficult to think about her, well, what happened to her."

"She was murdered," Melody said bluntly. She downed

what was left of her drink and then looked around the room, waving at the waitress when she spotted her. "I'll have another," she shouted at the woman. "Barry, you can pay for this one."

Barry nodded unenthusiastically.

No one spoke until after Melody's drink was delivered.

"Put it on my tab," Barry muttered.

Melody took a drink and then smiled as she slowly looked around the group. "I want to get to know you all in the same way that my mother did. Tell me all of your deepest, darkest secrets."

Barry laughed. "Your mother used to say things like that all the time. None of us have any deep or dark secrets, though. We're all just ordinary people with ordinary secrets."

"So start there," Melody suggested with a sly smile.

"I'm married but I have a boyfriend," Connie said, patting Ricky's knee.

Ricky laughed. "I'm having an affair with a married woman," he added.

"I don't have secrets," Neal said stiffly. "My life is an open book."

"What do you do for a living, Neal?" Melody asked.

"I'm the vice president of relationship management for Nightshade Bank, a subsidiary of..."

"Some massive conglomerate that owns more of the world than is fair or right," Melody interrupted. "Do you like banking?"

"I'm very successful at what I do. I can't imagine doing anything else," Neal told her.

"You have a very limited imagination," Melody replied.

As Neal flushed, Melody turned her attention to Joe. "And what do you do?" she asked.

"I work with computers," he replied.

"For whom?" Melody demanded.

"Scott Wright. He owns several small businesses in the area," Joe told her.

"Ah, yes, I want to meet him. I understand he knew my mother," Melody said.

"Everyone in Nightshade knew your mother," Barry told her. "And by the time she left, she knew everyone in Nightshade."

"And all of their secrets," Connie added.

Melody grinned. "Barry, I haven't heard any of your secrets."

He shrugged. "I drink too much to keep secrets. Once I start drinking, I'll tell anyone everything there is to know about me. It's sad, but true."

"That just leaves you," Melody said to Joe. "Tell me everything interesting about you."

Joe flushed and then drained what was left in his beer mug. "I'm not interesting enough to have secrets," he said. "And now I have to go."

He was sitting in the back of the circular booth, right in the middle of the group. Abigail was quick to jump up, happy to move from her uncomfortable perch. For a moment, no one else moved.

"Really," Joe said tightly.

Ricky and Connie slowly slid out of the booth, letting Joe out.

"We'll see you on Saturday," Neal said. "You don't want to miss the Halloween party."

"Yeah, right," Joe replied as he headed for the door.

"You're all going to be there, aren't you?" Abigail asked as Connie and Ricky returned to their seats.

"We are," Neal agreed. "I've tasked every member with the job of memorizing a single ghost story. That should give you enough stories to entertain your guests."

"I'm sure it will," Abigail replied.

"My friend Bob said he'd bring his horse and cart for hayrides," Barry told her.

"Don't let him," Connie said loudly. "His horse is older than I am and slow as anything. He'll take your guests a few hundred feet and then stop and fart for twenty minutes. Hayrides are a terrible idea, anyway. It's supposed to snow on Saturday."

"Is it?" Neal asked. "I hadn't realized."

"Maybe we won't bother with hayrides," Abigail said.

"The snow won't stick around, not this early in the year," Ricky said.

"But wouldn't it be wonderful if it did?" Melody asked. "I can just imagine all of us getting snowed in at the lodge, all dressed in our Halloween costumes. Imagine how much more terrifying the ghost stories would be if we were all trapped together in the lodge, unable to get away."

"It would be the perfect setting for a murder," Barry said.

"What a horrible idea," Melody said with a wicked grin. "Of course, it's entirely possible someone at this table has already murdered someone. I've heard that it gets easier after the first time."

"I think that's quite enough for tonight," Neal said stiffly. "Again, I'm sorry for your loss." He got to his feet and looked around the table. "Don't forget to learn your stories by heart. We want to make the best possible impression on Ms. Clark's guests."

"Thank you," Abigail said to Neal's departing back.

"I suppose that's our cue," Connie said. "No pun intended, fellow thespians."

She and Ricky slid back out of the booth. Ricky put his arm around her and then headed for the door.

"And then there was one," Melody said. She got up and sat down next to Barry. "You were my mother's lover. Tell me everything," she said in a low voice.

Barry flushed. "I don't know what to tell you. We had some fun together. I cared deeply about her. It didn't work out."

"What happened to end the relationship?" Melody asked.

"I wish I knew," Barry replied. "One day we were living together and the next day she moved out. She said she just wanted more space, but I knew that she was planning to end things."

"And then she disappeared," Melody said. "And you never filed a missing person report."

Barry sighed. "If I'd known or even suspected anything, of course I would have called the police, but I just assumed that she'd left town. I knew she was thinking about leaving. I had no reason to suspect that she'd — that she hadn't — that, anything."

Melody sighed. "The question is, would the police have found her if you had reported her missing? Would they have had any reason to look for her in the boathouse?"

"I can't imagine why she was there," Barry said. "It had been locked up for around five years by that point. She didn't have any reason to go there."

"But it was a quiet spot, away from prying eyes in a small town," Melody suggested.

"You think she had another man in her life," Barry said sadly.

"I don't know what to think," Melody countered. "But that's one possibility."

"I think I need to go home and get some sleep," Barry said, struggling to shift his body out from the corner of the booth.

Melody sat and watched as he worked his way out. She could have moved to give him a shorter distance to travel, but perhaps the idea didn't occur to her.

Abigail had been standing since Joe had left. Now she

looked at Melody. "Ready to go back to the lodge?" she asked hopefully as Barry shuffled out of the room.

"Absolutely," Melody replied.

Both women were silent on the drive back to the lodge. Abigail parked and then they walked back to the annex together.

"Thank you," Melody said. "All in all, I think that was a productive evening."

She disappeared into her room before Abigail could question the odd choice of words. As Abigail dug into her purse for her key, she thought better of it and turned and walked to the main building.

"Did you have a nice evening?" Arnold asked from behind the reception desk.

"Not at all," Abigail told him. "But I'm back now. I hope I didn't miss anything."

He shook his head. "Carl got 6A ready for the guests who were supposed to stay in 4A. He said that was the next best room."

"He's right, and he's wonderful for doing that. We should be all ready for our guests tomorrow, then."

"Are you excited about welcoming guests?"

Abigail thought about the question for a moment. "Actually, now that I think about it, I'm very excited. My sister and I talked about doing this for years, but I never actually thought we'd do it, not until very recently. I'm really excited that we're having our first themed weekend. I just hope everything goes to plan."

Arnold laughed. "You have plans with backup plans and backup to the backup plans. Things are going to be fine."

"I certainly hope so."

The pair chatted for a few more minutes before Abigail decided she was too tired to worry about her plans any longer.

"I'll see you in the morning," she said after a yawn.

Arnold nodded. "I may hang around in the lobby for a few hours tomorrow afternoon. I'm happy to help folks with their bags, and I'm eager to get a look at our guests."

"I just can't wait to see what everyone does for Halloween costumes."

"That's going to be interesting, too."

"Call me if you need me."

"I can't imagine why I'd need you, but I know where to find you if I do."

Back in her room in the annex, Abigail washed her face and then changed into her pajamas. She was worried that she might not sleep, but once her head hit the pillow, she was out.

"Carl can show you to your room," she said brightly to the young couple who were the first to arrive the next day.

Carl nodded as he walked out from behind the desk. "Happy to do it," he said. "Let me get that bag for you."

"I can manage," the male half of the couple said. "We can find our own room, too."

"Charles," the woman said in a low voice. "He's only trying to help."

"He's only trying to get himself a big tip," the man countered. "This weekend was expensive enough without having to fork out tips every time we turn around."

"I'm quite happy to carry your bag to your room without a tip," Carl told them. "We like to treat our guests like family, and my family certainly never tips me."

Both members of the couple were laughing as Carl picked up the largest of their suitcases and led them away.

"Did you get the Browns settled in?" Abigail asked when Carl returned a short while later.

"I did, and Mrs. Brown slipped me ten bucks while her husband wasn't looking."

"That was kind of her."

Carl nodded. "I truly don't care about tips. You pay me a fair wage for my work."

"But tips are always appreciated."

"Yes, of course."

The remainder of the afternoon seemed to fly past as the rest of the guests for Halloween weekend arrived. Abigail didn't see Melody until it was time for dinner.

"How are you?" she asked the woman as she walked into the dining room a few minutes before the meal was due to be served.

"I'm fine," Melody replied with a bright smile. "More than fine, really. Everything is good."

"I'm glad to hear that," Abigail replied. She was too busy with guests to question the woman's words.

Marcia's special first night meal was very well received. Abigail spent the dinner hour rushing back and forth to the kitchen, helping deliver food and drinks and grabbing her own meal in between.

"That was wonderful," she told Marcia after the last of the dessert dishes had been cleared away. Then she rushed back into the dining room.

"I hope you all enjoyed dinner. If you'd care to move into the lobby, we'll have drinks and snacks for you to enjoy around the fire during our social hour."

Carl and Arnold had everything in the lobby set up as the group arrived. Guests were given a choice of either warm apple cider or Arnold's Pumpkin Patch Punch, which was an instant hit. There were trays full of donuts and cookies for everyone to enjoy.

"What's in the punch?" Abigail asked after the guests had all been served.

Arnold stirred the orange mixture and grinned at her. "Orange sherbet, lemon-lime soda, a bit of rum and a few secret ingredients."

"Is it good?"

He laughed. "I can hear the doubt in your voice, but it's actually quite tasty." He used a ladle to pour some into a glass that he held out toward her.

"I don't drink when we have guests," she said.

"You'd have to drink the entire punch bowl to feel any effect," he replied. "There's barely any rum in there."

She took the glass and took a small sip. "It is good," she said. "It's a bit too sweet for me, but it's good."

Arnold nodded. "It is sweet, but the guests seem to like it."

Abigail stood with Arnold and Carl and watched as the guests slowly began to chat with one another. An hour later, they were all talking like old friends, laughing together while everyone talked about their children and grandchildren.

"They're getting along well," Arnold said in a low voice.

Abigail nodded. "Surprisingly well, really."

The words were barely out of her mouth when the front door swung open.

"Good evening," Jessica said as she walked into the room. "I didn't realize you were having a party. I was hoping to talk to Melody for a short while."

"Have some punch," Arnold suggested.

"And then come and sit next to me," Melody called from her seat on one of the sofas. "You can tell me all of your secrets."

Jessica laughed. "We don't have enough time for that, not tonight. I'll have to limit myself to the highlights."

"I can't wait," Melody replied with a laugh.

Jessica carried a glass of punch over to the sofa and sat down next to Melody. Abigail watched the pair for several minutes, wondering what they were discussing as they seemed to be whispering back and forth together. The other guests all appeared to be happy enough to ignore the two women and the low buzz of their conversation made it impossible for Abigail to make out anything that Melody and Jessica were saying, even after she'd slowly made her way closer and closer to the pair.

The social hour was supposed to be just that, an hour, but it was nearly midnight when Abigail decided that she'd had enough. She wanted to get some sleep and she needed her guests out of the way so that she and her staff could clean up the mess.

"Okay, folks, I'm sorry to say it, but we need to wrap things up for tonight. Remember that tomorrow is our Halloween party. We're going to have a group of actors from the town here to share ghost stories with you, along with other Halloween entertainment. Don't forget to wear your costumes. There will be prizes for the best ones," she announced as Marcia began to clear away the remains of the treats they'd offered.

A few people grumbled as they got to their feet, but the room cleared of nearly all of the guests in less than five minutes. Only Melody remained, looking as if she had no intention of leaving her seat next to Jessica.

Abigail helped clear away the last of the punch and then started going around the room collecting empty glasses, mugs, and plates. Thanks to Carl and Arnold and Marcia, that job didn't take long at all.

"I'm going to load the dishwasher and then head for home," Marcia told her. "I'll start it running when I come back to make breakfast."

"Whatever works for you," Abigail replied. She walked over to where Jessica and Melody were sitting. "It's getting late," she said.

Jessica nodded. "I think we're nearly done," she said. "You go and get some sleep. Arnold can look after us."

Abigail sighed and then walked over to the reception desk. Arnold had taken a seat behind it.

"They aren't going anywhere in a hurry," she told him.

He shrugged. "They can keep me company, then. It doesn't matter to me."

"I should stay."

"You should go," Carl told her as he joined them. "You're going to have a very busy day tomorrow. You need to be at your best."

"He's not wrong," Arnold said. "You have staff so that you don't have to do everything yourself, right?"

"You're right, but ultimately the lodge is my responsibility," she replied.

"But it's our home, too," Arnold reminded her. "And we want it to succeed as much as you do."

With those words ringing in her ears, Abigail walked back to the annex and went to bed.

Chapter Thirteen

"Happy Halloween," Marcia said as Abigail walked into the dining room the next morning.

"Happy Halloween," she replied as she poured herself a cup of coffee. She took a slow sip and then waited for the caffeine to have an effect. After another sip, she gave up waiting for a miracle and resigned herself to being overtired for the day.

"Arnold said he had a quiet night," Marcia told her when she brought in her breakfast a few minutes later.

"Yes, he told me the same thing. Apparently, our guests all went to bed and stayed there. So far they're model guests, really."

"We try," a voice said from the doorway.

Abigail smiled brightly at the young couple who walked into the dining room. "Good morning and happy Halloween."

The woman giggled. "I love Halloween. I hope it's okay that I'm already in costume."

"Of course it's okay. I'll be running a shuttle back and forth to town today so that you can see some of what Nightshade has to offer. I'm sure some of the shop keepers and residents will be in costume, too," Abigail replied, mentally crossing her fingers and hoping she was right.

A few minutes later, the dining room was full of guests. Nearly all of them were in costume, and they were quick to talk excitedly together about the day ahead.

"I just want to spend the whole day in the bookstore," one woman said. "I looked it up online. It's full of old books and new books and everything in between."

Abigail nodded. "Nightshade Books is a wonderful store. You could spend several days there, wandering from shelf to shelf, and still not see everything. I try to get down there whenever I have a free afternoon."

As the small group began to discuss favorite books, Abigail excused herself. She carried her half-eaten plate of food into the kitchen, where Marcia was hard at work on the preparations for dinner.

"While we have guests, it might be best if I eat in here," she said, putting her plate on the counter and dropping onto a stool.

"Janet used to eat in here when they had guests. Sometimes she'd eat at the reception desk. She didn't really like having guests, though. Jack loved it. He used to try to make sure he ate at the busiest possible times, so he could be surrounded by guests."

"I didn't realize that Janet didn't enjoy having guests."

"She didn't mind them, but she preferred not to spend too much of her time with them," Marcia clarified.

Abigail finished her breakfast and then slipped her plate into the dishwasher. "I need to go and get the van ready. I'm going to be taking folks back and forth to town today."

"Make sure they all visit the bookstore and the candy store."

"Those are on my list of suggestions, along with the store

that sells things made by local crafters, and QuackMart just for the name."

Marcia laughed. "We're all so used to having QuackMart that we never think about how it must sound to outsiders. Let me know if I can help in any way."

"I'm pretty sure you have your hands full here."

"I'm just about finished with the prep work. Once everyone has finished breakfast, I'll have a few hours to put my feet up before I need to actually start cooking dinner."

"Once I get the first lot of guests delivered downtown, I'll start cleaning rooms. I hope no one has left me too much of a mess."

"People can be incredibly messy when they're on vacation. I'm always very careful to clean up after myself when I travel. I even make my own bed when I'm staying in a hotel."

Abigail laughed. "I don't expect people to make their own beds, but I don't have a lot of time to get the rooms done in between trips into town."

"I'm sure Carl can do some of the driving."

"That's my backup plan."

Half an hour later, Abigail had made her first trip into town, dropping off a handful of guests. When she got back to the lodge, the rest of the guests, including Melody, were having breakfast.

"The van into town will leave from the front door in half an hour," she told everyone. Then she dashed up the stairs and dragged out the cleaning cart.

The rest of the day seemed to be one large blur of cleaning and driving guests back and forth to Nightshade. It was nearly time for dinner before she finally returned to the lodge with the last of the guests.

"I bought so many books," one of the women said as they all walked inside together. "I don't have enough room in my suitcase for this many books." Her large bag was full to the top with hardcovers.

"We could have ordered them all online," her husband said. "That would have been cheaper and easier."

"Yes, but this way we supported a small independent bookstore," his wife countered. "And I got immediate gratification."

"Dinner will be served in ten minutes," Abigail announced as the guests all headed for the stairs. "The party will start shortly after dinner." She stuck her head into the kitchen to make sure that everything was going to plan before she rushed back to her room to get ready for dinner. There wouldn't be time to change between the meal and the party, so she pulled on her Halloween costume and then brushed her brown bob into a ponytail.

"It will have to do," she muttered as she studied her reflection.

She didn't have the time or the skill to do her makeup the way that Wolfram Woman had done hers in the movie, but it didn't really matter. The costume was immediately identifiable.

The guests were all gathering in the lobby when Abigail returned. She walked around the room, admiring costumes as she went. Melody was standing by herself in a corner.

"That's a beautiful dress," Abigail said as she approached her.

"Thanks. Like I said, my mother made it for me years ago," Melody replied, running a hand along her skirt.

"She did beautiful work."

"She did, and now she's gone, and I'm really struggling with, well, life right now."

"I'm sorry. Is there anything I can do?"

Melody shrugged. "I don't know how much of the party

I'm going to attend. I may sneak away after dinner and just go to bed."

"That's fine. If you need anything, just ask."

"Thanks."

Dinner was a huge success. Abigail ate in the kitchen while the guests ate in the dining room.

"I'd almost forgotten what it feels like to have guests," Marcia remarked as she rushed back and forth. "If we had a few more, we'd have to do dinner in two sittings."

"We may need to do that for Thanksgiving. A lot will depend on how much work the rooms on the third and fourth floor need. They're my next priority."

"I thought maybe you'd work on the cottages next."

"I thought about it, but I think we're more likely to get guests who want to stay in the main lodge than guests who want to stay in the cottages at this time of year. I know the cottages all have heating, but I suspect they are all cold and drafty anyway."

"Jack and Janet rarely rented them out in the colder months," Marcia told her. "As you say, they are all cold and drafty. You may want to look into adding some better insulation to them before you do much else."

Abigail sighed. "That's another expense, though. It might be easier and cheaper to just leave them empty for now."

The Nightshade Players began to arrive while Abigail was eating her dessert. She got Marcia to give them all dinner in the kitchen before the party.

"How are you?" she asked Barry as he sat down next to her.

He was dressed like a pirate, with a patch over one eye and a stuffed parrot on his shoulder. "I don't know," he replied. "I just wish Helena was here. I've been missing her for five years, and now I miss her even more."

Abigail patted his hand. "I'm sorry for your loss."

"I wish the police would hurry up and figure out what happened to her. It's hard, not knowing."

"She probably got drunk and climbed into the boat to sleep it off," Neal suggested. "Maybe she hit her head as she climbed in."

"Someone murdered her," Barry replied tightly.

"I can't see how they can be so certain after all this time," Joe said. "I mean, all they have to go on is a skeleton, right?"

Connie shivered. "I want to be cremated. I don't want anyone finding my bones years later. As soon as I'm dead, burn me up and put me in an urn."

"Maybe Helena wanted to be cremated, too," Ricky said.

"But if I suddenly disappeared, you'd find me," Connie replied. "You wouldn't leave me locked in a boathouse for five years."

"I still don't understand why Jack and Janet never found the body," Barry said. Everyone in the room looked at Abigail.

"I've no idea. They just said that they'd locked it up after one summer and never bothered to open the door again. Apparently, they'd decided that the boat rental business was more trouble than it was worth," she told them.

"I can't believe Jack didn't try to sell the boats that were left," Barry said. "As I understand it, he and Janet were really struggling financially in the end."

"I'm sure the police have asked them all of those questions and more," Abigail said. "And now it's nearly time for the party. Are you all ready with your stories?"

"Yes, of course," Neal said. "We're professionals, after all."

Abigail nodded and then walked with the little group into the lobby. Guests were standing around in clusters, holding drinks and chatting together. Carl had dimmed the lighting, allowing a few strategically placed candles to cast odd shadows in every corner. Abigail shivered as she crossed the floor.

"Good evening," Neal said in a creepy tone. His vampire

costume seemed to suit him as he twirled in his cape and then began to slowly walk around the room. "Do you believe in ghosts?" he asked one young woman.

She hesitated and then shook her head.

Neal laughed. "How foolish of you. Ghosts are everywhere, of course. Let me tell you a story about something that happened in this very lodge not so many years ago."

Guests crowded closer to Neal as he began his story. Abigail walked over to the table holding drinks and poured herself some apple cider.

"Good evening," Jessica said as she joined Abigail.

"You look lovely," Abigail said, admiring the beautiful vintage wedding gown the other woman was wearing.

Jessica shrugged. "It's my own dress. I got married in it many, many years ago. As it still fits and no one in my family is interested in ever wearing it for anything, I thought it was perfect for Halloween."

"It's gorgeous."

"It was quite expensive back in the day, but it's held up well. I never imagined, back then, that I'd find an excuse to wear it nearly sixty years after my wedding."

"It's really beautiful."

"I had an interesting conversation with Janet today."

"Janet Johnstone? Did you ask her about the boathouse?"

Jessica nodded. "As I said, it was an interesting conversation."

"Tell me everything."

"I don't want you to accuse me of sticking my nose into a police investigation, though."

"You've already done that. I just want to know what you found out."

Jessica chuckled. "I mustn't tease, really. Let's start with why they decided to stop renting out boats, shall we?"

"Sure, why did they stop renting out boats?"

"Because Janet had a bad dream."

Abigail stared at her. "I wasn't expecting that. Are you serious?"

Jessica nodded. "It wasn't anything prophetic or anything. She just had a nightmare about falling into the water when she was walking to the boathouse. You know how the path goes quite close to the lake in some areas? She dreamt that she and Jack both fell into the water and couldn't get out."

"I can see why that would be scary."

"From what Janet said, Jack didn't need much persuading to stay away from the boathouse. Boat rentals had never made them much money, and the upkeep on the boats and the boathouse took a lot of effort. Janet was the one who always liked being able to offer the rentals to their guests. Once she'd decided that she and Jack needed to stay away from the building, Jack never bothered to visit again."

"How did he know that he didn't have the right key, then?"

"When they first listed the property for sale, a few years ago, the realtor who listed it went down to the boathouse with the keys that Jack had. He couldn't get into the boathouse. Apparently, Jack looked everywhere, but couldn't find any other keys."

"Which suggests that the lock that was on the boathouse wasn't the one that Jack put on it ten years ago," Abigail said thoughtfully.

"It seems most likely to me that whoever killed Helena put a new lock on the door. The killer probably knew that Jack and Janet would never bother trying to get inside the building again."

"Now I wish I'd insisted on seeing the inside of the boathouse when we first toured the property."

"But then you would have been stuck in Nightshade for a while during the police investigation while you were still living and working in New York City," Jessica pointed out. "At least now you already live here."

"I suppose."

"I do hope you aren't talking about an active criminal investigation," a voice interrupted.

Abigail smiled at Greg Trushell as he joined them. "We were just chatting," she said. "Ready to play some spooky music?"

He nodded. "I have everything set up. I just wanted to check with you to see when you want me to start."

"After this ghost story, I think," Abigail replied. "You can play for half an hour or so, and then we'll have another ghost story."

Greg nodded. "Do you want people to dance?"

Abigail shrugged. "I don't mind either way. There are a few people in the crowd who seem like they might want to dance – to the right music, anyway."

"I'll put some definite dance music in the first set and see how it goes," Greg told her. "Feel free to come over at any point to request different things, though. I want to give you the party you want."

Abigail smiled at him. "I just want our guests to be happy. This is our first themed weekend, but I'm hoping it won't be our last."

Greg nodded. "I'll be behind my table, finalizing my selections. Give me a sign when the story finishes."

"It should be nearly done," Abigail said, turning to look at Neal who appeared to have everyone hanging on his every word.

"So after all of that, Jack and Janet couldn't really help," Abigail said to Jessica as Greg walked away.

"Janet did say something else that was interesting," Jessica replied. "She told me that about five years ago, she started to think that someone was using the boathouse late at night."

"Using the boathouse? What does that mean?"

"At the time, she thought it was probably kids looking for a place to smoke or drink or, well, you know. She noticed that the path appeared trampled down more than usual one day when she was walking on the beach. She told me that she heard voices, too, once in a while, voices that seemed to be coming from the direction of the boathouse."

"The boathouse is pretty far away from the lodge. I'd be surprised if she could hear voices at that distance."

"She heard them when she was walking on the beach, not from the lodge," Jessica explained. "Janet liked to walk on the beach, sometimes late at night. She told me that she heard voices in the evenings, often after midnight, when her insomnia was keeping her up."

"But she didn't investigate any further?"

Jessica shook her head. "She said she didn't much care what was going on at the boathouse. I gather she and Jack had some insurance on the building and its contents. I don't think either of them would have been disappointed if it had suddenly burned to the ground."

"And that was about five years ago?"

"To the best of Janet's recollection. It's possible she has the dates wrong, of course. But it fits with the timeline we already have. Maybe Helena was using the boathouse as a rendezvous spot with one of her lovers."

"Why would she use a more or less abandoned boathouse for any reason? Surely there were plenty of other places around town where she could meet people."

"Maybe, but the boathouse gave her total privacy."

"Except for when Janet was strolling on the beach. She would have seen anyone coming or going to the boathouse, wouldn't she?"

"If she'd hung around on the beach, sure, but she told me

she never bothered to do so. She didn't really care what was going on at the boathouse after dark."

Abigail sighed. "I can't help but wish that she and Jack had kept a closer eye on the boathouse. They could have saved me a lot of aggravation."

"And all that's left is a dismembered hand." Neal's voice filled the room as he reached into a pocket and pulled out a fake plastic hand. A few people jumped and one woman screamed while Neal chuckled and waved the hand at them.

"Thank you, Neal," Abigail said as people began to get up from the couches and head for the table full of food and drinks. "And now DJ GT is going to entertain us with some of the best spooky music out there."

Greg picked up the microphone on the table in front of him and introduced himself before starting the first song. As *Monster Mash* filled the room, Abigail sat down next to Neal.

"That was very good," she told him. "Just what the party needed."

He nodded. "The others all have stories, too, but I do think mine was the best."

Of course you do, Abigail thought. "I suppose we'll have to see how the evening goes," she said. "In the meantime, get yourself a drink or a snack."

He nodded and then slowly rose to his feet. A quick twirl made his cape swirl around him. He grabbed the edges and waved them dramatically. "Of course, it would never do to reveal my bat form here," he said loudly. "It is tempting, though."

Abigail watched as he turned and strolled through the crowd. Her guests all seemed to step back to make room for him as he made his way to the table full of food and drinks. A few people had decided that the spot in front of the DJ was the perfect dance floor, and they were happily bopping to the music, drinks in hand.

As the first notes of *Thriller* played over the sound system, Abigail did a quick head count, making sure that all of her guests were accounted for. Melody and Jessica were talking together in the corner. As Abigail headed toward them, Melody stood up and made a beeline for Neal.

Chapter Fourteen

Abigail sighed and then walked quickly toward Neal. It wasn't that she didn't trust Melody and Jessica – okay, it was totally that she didn't trust Melody and Jessica. It seemed likely that the two were up to no good, and Abigail didn't want anything to interrupt her Halloween party.

"...should know," Melody was saying when Abigail reached them.

"Yes, well, thank you for that," Neal replied. He looked over at Abigail and frowned. "I don't know that I'm going to stay much longer. I've done my part, of course. You don't mind if I leave shortly, do you?"

"Ah, but Neal, you'll miss all of the excitement," Melody told him. "Jessica and I have something special planned for later."

Abigail frowned. "I think we need to talk," she said to Melody.

Neal chuckled. "I don't think Abigail is going to approve of your plans," he said.

Melody shrugged. "They're Jessica's plans. I'm just trying

to help her. It isn't anything important, though. If Abigail doesn't approve, we'll settle for listening to more ghost stories for tonight."

"And I've already told my story," Neal said. "I've no reason to stay."

Melody looked at him for a moment. "If I were you, I'd stick around," she said, staring into his eyes as she spoke.

Neal flushed. "I have a headache."

"I'm sure Abigail can give you something," Melody replied.

"Of course," Abigail said. "What do you prefer?"

"Or what's your poison?" Melody asked with a slightly sinister laugh.

Neal flushed. "I'm fine. I'll stay for as long as I can, but don't be surprised if I slip away unannounced."

"I might not be surprised, but I'll be disappointed," Melody told him before she turned and walked away.

"Would you like something for your headache?" Abigail asked Neal, who was frowning at Melody's back.

He shook his head. "As I said, I may just slip away while everyone is busy doing other things. Joe's ghost story is excellent and should draw everyone's attention. No one will notice if I sneak out while he's telling it."

"You're all here as volunteers. I'm thrilled that you were willing to help out. You're more than welcome to leave whenever it suits you."

"Yes, well, we'll see," Neal replied, his eyes still on Melody.

Abigail followed his gaze and saw that Melody was now talking to Joe. Whatever she was saying, it appeared to be making Joe uncomfortable. He was frowning and shaking his head while she spoke.

"It seems very much as if Melody is trying to spoil your party," Neal said. "Perhaps you should ask her to leave."

"I may just do that," Abigail muttered as she turned and

walked briskly toward Melody and Joe. Melody saw her coming and quickly whispered something into Joe's ear before spinning on her heel and walking briskly to the food table.

"Is everyone okay?" Abigail asked Joe when she reached him.

He shrugged. "I'm just nervous about my story, really. Melody was trying to give me some pointers, but I'm afraid they fell on deaf ears."

"Really? Does she know a lot about acting and storytelling?"

Joe flushed. "She was just assuring me that no one would care if I messed everything up and forgot the ending or whatever. She reminded me that no one here is going to be able to advance my acting career, so I don't need to take the job too seriously."

"She's right. My guests are all just ordinary people who wanted to celebrate Halloween. Are you hoping to become a famous actor one day, then?"

"Who isn't?" Joe replied. "I mean, if someone walked in here right now and offered you a starring role in a Hollywood blockbuster, you'd take it, wouldn't you?"

Abigail thought for a moment. "Actually, probably not. Acting isn't something I want to do. I expect I'd be terrible and get fired after the first day, anyway."

Joe shrugged. "It's all I've ever wanted to do. I wanted to try my luck in California years ago, but circumstances kept me here. I keep telling myself it isn't too late, but I'm also terrified of failure."

"Surely Scott would let you take a leave of absence to give it a try."

"Maybe, but I don't think that's what I'd want to do. If I'm going to go and try to find fame and fortune, I'd rather not have anything to fall back on. I'd rather have no choice but to fight for my opportunities."

"For now, maybe you could just tell a ghost story," Abigail suggested as Greg finished another track.

Joe nodded. "I'm ready for my cue."

Abigail crossed to the DJ. "Time for another ghost story," she told him.

He nodded and then made an announcement. The guests all gathered back at the couches, seemingly eager to hear another story. Joe watched them from a distance, not joining them until everyone was seated.

"Witches are fascinating creatures," he said as he sat down in the center of the group. "Fascinating and deadly."

Abigail shivered and then deliberately tuned out the rest of the story. While all of the guests were being entertained, she helped Marcia and Carl refill the plates and punch bowls on the food table. On her way back from the kitchen, carrying a tray full of finger foods, she spotted Melody and Jessica talking together in the far corner of the room.

"Those two are up to something," she muttered.

Marcia followed her gaze and then shrugged. "At least they're keeping each other busy. Goodness only knows what either of them would get up to if she got bored."

Abigail grinned. "There is that. I can't help but worry that they're planning to interfere in the police investigation, though."

"It's a Halloween party. What could they possibly do here?" Marcia asked.

Abigail looked around the room, her eyes seeing potential dangers everywhere. "Just keep an eye on them for me," she told Marcia. "And ask Carl and Arnold to do the same. I don't want either of them starting a scene or making any crazy accusations."

Marcia nodded. "Now that you've mentioned it, that seems uncomfortably possible."

"...into a toad." Joe said, pulling a small toad out of his pocket.

A few people shrieked as the animal looked around and then jumped out of Joe's hand and onto the floor. Joe laughed as he scooped the angry animal up and then got to his feet.

"I'll just drop him back outside," he said. "He'll find his way back to the lake in no time."

As Joe walked to the door, Melody followed, standing in the doorway, and silently watching whatever Joe did outside. They had a short conversation when he returned before he shut the door behind himself and looked around the room.

"Is there somewhere that I can wash my hands?" he asked Abigail a moment later.

"Sure, there's a bathroom behind that door," she replied, pointing.

Melody still seemed to be watching Joe closely as the man disappeared into the bathroom. Before Abigail could question her about her fixation, the DJ started playing music again. Within half a minute, it seemed as if all of the guests, including Melody, were dancing.

"Great party," a voice said in Abigail's ear.

"Barry, I'm glad you're having fun," she replied as she turned around to face the man.

He shrugged. "I'd be having more fun if I could have a drink or two, but I don't dare do that until after I've told my story. Neal will have a fit if I forget half of it because I've been drinking."

"Are you next?"

"I certainly hope so," Barry laughed. "We didn't really talk about what order we were going to go in, but then I didn't know there was going to be anything to drink here, either. If I'd known that, I'd have insisted on going first."

"The DJ is going to do about twenty minutes of music, and then it will be time for another story."

"Yeah, my story, even if I have to talk over everyone else to make it happen."

"Barry, there you are," Melody said as she joined them. "I was hoping to have a little chat with you."

Barry frowned. "Now? I mean, I'm happy to talk to you, but I'm really focused on remembering my story right now. Can we talk after I'm done?"

Melody laughed lightly. "Of course, darling. I'd hate to make you forget anything important. Just don't leave tonight without talking to me. Promise?"

"Of course."

Melody winked at him and then walked away, heading toward Ricky and Connie, who were standing together near the DJ.

"She's up to no good," Barry muttered.

"Melody?"

"Yeah. I'm not sure what she's doing, but I don't trust her."

"She seems to be trying to talk to everyone in the Nightshade Players."

"It's what she's saying that worries me."

"Maybe you should have talked to her and gotten it out of the way."

"Maybe, but I meant what I said. I need to concentrate on my story. Whatever Melody wants, I'd bet my last dollar it's going to be upsetting."

Abigail turned and watched as Melody whispered something into Ricky's ear. The man frowned and then nodded before following Melody across the room toward the door.

"Connie isn't happy," Barry said, nodding toward his wife.

Connie was staring at Ricky, a frown on her face.

Abigail sighed. "At least the guests are having fun," she said before she started walking toward Melody and Ricky.

"Ah, Abigail, hello," a loud voice said before Abigail had made it very far.

"Hello, Jessica."

"It's a lovely party," Jessica told her. "All of your guests seem to be having a wonderful time."

"I hope so. The music is good, and the stories have been well done."

"Indeed. I thought they were both just right. A little bit scary but a little bit funny as well. Who is next?"

"I believe Barry, but I'm not sure about that."

"I wonder if any of your guests would like a chance to tell a story."

Abigail frowned. "I never thought of that."

"You may want to ask them, maybe after Barry's turn."

"Yes, that's a good point. I probably should ask them."

"I suspect Melody knows a few ghost stories."

"She might, but I feel as if she has more on her mind tonight than ghost stories."

Jessica shrugged. "She's trying to talk to all of the Nightshade Players. She wants to hear every story she can about her mother's time in Nightshade. I believe she's feeling guilty for not reporting her mother missing five years ago."

"She can't blame herself for that."

"Which is exactly what I told her, but I don't think she believed me." Jessica sighed. "She may feel better once the police work out exactly what happened to Helena."

"I just hope she's leaving the investigation to the police."

Jessica's eyes went wide. "Whatever do you mean?"

"You know exactly what I mean, and I hope you aren't encouraging Melody to question everyone. Someone has gotten away with murder for five years. He or she must be hoping to avoid detection now."

"Whoever killed Helena deserves to go to prison for a very long time."

THE BODY IN THE BOATHOUSE

"Yes, but it's up to the police to find that person. I hope you aren't interfering again."

"As if I would."

Abigail stared at the older woman. "I don't have time to keep an eye on Melody tonight."

"I'll take care of Melody. You worry about your other guests."

Abigail had a lot more she wanted to say, but she didn't get a chance as Ricky joined them and took Abigail's arm.

"We need to talk," he said angrily as he led her away from the others.

"What's wrong?" Abigail asked as Ricky rushed her into the corridor behind the lobby.

"That woman is making all sorts of crazy accusations," he said.

"Melody?"

"Yes, Melody. She more or less accused me of murdering her mother. When I laughed, she told me that she knew her mother had been blackmailing me, and she knew why. I think she was expecting me to offer her money, but I just laughed again. I barely knew Helena Lane. She certainly wasn't blackmailing me, and I definitely didn't kill her."

"I'm sorry," Abigail replied with a sigh. "I think Melody is desperate to work out what happened to her mother. She's saying things that she thinks might get a reaction, regardless of the danger. I'll talk to her."

"I can believe that her mother was blackmailing people," Ricky said.

"Oh?"

"She lived better than she should have, even if she was the most popular waitress at the diner. I know what apartments in The Towers go for, and there's no way she could have afforded to live there on what a waitress makes."

"She did only live there for a short while, though, didn't she?"

"She only stayed there for a short while, but she kept the apartment, even after she moved in with Barry," Ricky told her. "I think she told Barry that she'd given it up, but I know someone who lives there, and he told me that Helena still had her apartment. He used to see her going in and out at odd times, presumably when Barry was otherwise occupied."

"Do you really think she was blackmailing someone?"

Ricky shrugged. "It never really crossed my mind until Melody said what she said. Then it was like a piece of the puzzle slid into place and everything started to make sense. Helena lived above her means, and she was murdered. That sounds like blackmail to me."

Abigail was still thinking about his words as Ricky walked away, back to the party. When she returned to the lobby, she headed straight for Melody, who was talking to Connie.

"We need to talk," she said to Melody when she reached the women.

"Now?" Melody asked.

"Yes, now."

Melody sighed and then looked at Connie. "Remember what I said," she told her before she followed Abigail across the room.

"Ricky said you accused him of murder and told him that you knew your mother was blackmailing him," Abigail said as soon as the two women were in the corridor alone together.

"My goodness, he didn't waste any time complaining about me," Melody replied. "I suppose that makes him seem innocent, although I'm not sure he is."

"Was your mother blackmailing someone in Nightshade?"

Melody sighed. "I don't know," she admitted. "Mom was good at finding out people's secrets. People liked confiding in her. Of course, I'd be shocked and appalled to learn that she was using that to blackmail people."

"You don't sound terribly shocked or appalled," Abigail said dryly.

Melody shrugged. "Mom worked hard her entire life. If people sometimes gave her a bit of money to keep quiet about things they'd told her, that was her business."

"Blackmail is dangerous."

"Clearly, because it probably got her killed," Melody replied. "She never stayed in one place for very long. I assume, if she ever did blackmail anyone, that she got some money from them and then left town."

"You assume."

"Look, my mother's life was her business. All I'm doing is talking to people and hoping that one of them will admit that they killed her. Jessica suggested it."

"Jessica suggested that you set yourself up as a target for the killer?"

Melody shrugged. "Jessica suggested that I tell everyone that I know that my mother was blackmailing them."

"Does Jessica think your mother was blackmailing people?"

"It's possible, maybe even likely," Melody said with a frown. "My mother had a post office box. It isn't in her name, but it was her box. She left the key with me, and I still go and empty it every week or so."

"And it's full of payments from people being blackmailed?"

"I don't know that for a fact. Maybe the money that is sent there is to thank my mother for her friendship, or maybe some of it comes from some sort of pension plan that she set up somewhere."

"Your mother was blackmailing people all over the country

and you're still getting payments now. What's going to happen when people find out your mother is dead?"

"I'm more worried about finding out who killed her than anything else."

"Was she blackmailing people in Nightshade?"

"She may have been. I still get some payments from folks here."

"Which folks?"

Melody shrugged. "I've no idea. All of the payments are made with money orders that are anonymous and untraceable. I only know that they're coming from Nightshade because of the postmarks."

"And what did the police say when you told them all of this?"

"I can't very well tell them all of this, can I?" Melody demanded. "What my mother was doing might not have been strictly legal."

"No, of course not. I can't believe you're telling me about it." Abigail frowned. *The woman couldn't possibly be planning to kill her, could she?*

"If you tell the police, I'll simply deny everything," Melody said with a shrug. "Right now, the most important thing is finding out who killed my mother. I'll worry about the rest later."

Abigail thought for a minute. "What you need to do is find someone who paid your mother something five years ago, but then didn't pay any more money," she said eventually. "Someone who knew that they were no longer going to be blackmailed."

Melody stared at her. "That's brilliant. I should have kept better records. I need to talk to everyone again, to tell each of them that I know they stopped paying. That's much smarter than what I've been doing."

"You need to talk to the police," Abigail countered. "Tell

them that you've only just discovered what your mother was doing. They can investigate properly."

"But that will take ages. It will be much faster if I simply confront the suspects and see which one gives himself or herself away."

"You aren't giving them enough credit as actors."

"Please, have you seen them out there, telling ghost stories badly? None of them are proper actors. If I tell them that I know they stopped paying because they knew my mother was dead, one of them will do or say something that gives the game away. And then we can call the police with the name of the killer."

"It's dangerous."

"It's a party. There are over a dozen people in there, having fun, including a policeman acting as DJ. I couldn't be much safer."

"I still think you should call Fred and tell him everything."

"I'll tell Fred what he needs to know to put my mother's killer behind bars. Nothing else is any of his business."

"You never reported your mother missing because you were collecting all of the money from her various blackmail schemes," Abigail said as the idea occurred to her.

"I didn't report her missing because I thought she'd decided to go and live off the grid for a while. I did collect the money, but I put nearly all of it into a savings account. I assumed that one day my mother would surface and want the cash."

"What are you going to do with the money now?"

Melody grinned. "I understand you can retire to Mexico inexpensively. I think I'll buy a little house down there and simply sit in the sun sipping margaritas for the rest of my days."

"And now I believe it's time for another ghost story."

Abigail frowned as she heard the DJ's announcement.

"Please be careful," she said to Melody. "Someone in there may well have murdered your mother."

"I'm counting on that," Melody said. "She told me that the Nightshade Players were an untapped gold mine of misdeeds. I suspect she may well have been blackmailing all of them."

Abigail was still frowning as she followed Melody back into the lobby. The guests were clustered on the sofas around Barry, clearly eager for the next story. Melody walked over and stopped a few feet away from the group. She glanced at her watch and then looked around the room.

"What's going on?" Jessica hissed in Abigail's ear as she joined.

"Melody is determined to tell everyone that she knows that her mother was blackmailing them," Abigail replied. "And I'm afraid she's going to get herself killed in the process."

"It's a party," Jessica argued. "What could possibly go wrong?"

The words had barely left her lips when Abigail heard a loud crashing noise. A moment later, all of the lights went out. The candles that had been casting shadows had all either burned out or been extinguished. The room was pitch black.

Chapter Fifteen

Someone screamed. Abigail shut her eyes and then opened them again, hoping that would help them adjust to the sudden darkness.

"It's only a power failure," Carl's voice said loudly. "We have a backup generator. It just takes a minute or two to start."

As Abigail waited for the generator to come to life, she began to walk slowly toward Melody. If Carl was right, and it was just a power failure, then Melody was probably fine. If he was wrong, though, and something more sinister was happening, then Melody could be in danger.

"Everyone stay where they are," she said as she walked slowly and cautiously forward, one hand reaching into her pocket for her phone.

Across the room, someone held up his cell phone as a flashlight. "Turn it off," a voice called. The man laughed and then switched off the light.

"Now this is proper Halloween atmosphere," one of the guests said excitedly.

"Now this is dangerous," Abigail muttered. She took

another step toward where Melody had been standing and then stopped. Pulling out her phone, she tapped on the screen.

"Is everyone okay in here?" a voice said as the front door swung open. Arnold and his wife, Karen, walked in, each carrying a large flashlight. As they flashed the lights around the room, Abigail gasped. Joe was standing next to Melody with a knife in his hand.

"Melody, run!" she screamed.

Arnold turned his light on Melody as Abigail heard something hit the ground. Joe took a few steps backward and then began to walk toward the door.

"Where's the knife?" Abigail demanded.

"What knife?" Arnold asked.

"Joe had a knife," she explained.

"This is getting good now," one of the guests said. "Was someone murdered? Do we have to find the body and work out who killed them?"

"I hope no one was murdered," Abigail replied. "But I think someone nearly was. Stop Joe," she told Arnold.

"I was just going to see if I could get the generator started," Joe said. "It should have come on by now."

"I'll go and take a look," Carl said. He borrowed Karen's flashlight and disappeared through the door.

"Maybe you should finish your story," someone said to Barry.

Barry shook his head. "I think we have bigger problems right now," he muttered as he slid down in his seat.

"I'd like everyone to get his or her phone out and switch on the flashlight," Abigail announced. She turned her light on and swept the light along the floor next to Melody. The knife had fallen or been pushed partly under a couch.

"No one touch the knife," she said as she walked toward it. "I think everyone should move away from it, though."

"If I could have everyone's attention," Greg said in a loud

voice. "I'd like you all to stay exactly where you are. Just sit tight for a few minutes and we'll get the power back on and get things sorted out."

He walked over to Abigail. "Tell me what you saw," he said in a low voice.

"Joe had a knife in his hand, and he was standing behind Melody. She's been going around telling everyone that she knew her mother had been blackmailing them. I warned her that she was going to make herself a target, but she didn't listen."

Greg frowned. "Fred is on his way. Are you certain Joe had the knife in his hand?"

"Absolutely."

"I couldn't see any of that from where I was sitting," he explained. "Hopefully, we'll get fingerprints off the knife."

"Except Joe is wearing gloves," Abigail replied with a sigh. "They're part of his costume."

Greg looked around the room. "I'd like you all to take seats, those of you who are standing."

"I'm going to go and help Carl with the generator," Joe said. "Otherwise we may be in the dark all night."

"Sorry, but you need to stay here," Greg told him. "No one is going anywhere right now."

Joe frowned. "You don't actually believe that I had a knife, do you? I mean, I don't know what Abigail thought she saw, but I know I haven't done anything wrong."

"There is a knife on the floor near where you were standing," Greg said.

"Maybe it's a prop knife, something from someone's costume," Joe replied. "Whatever it is, it's nothing to do with me. I'd like to leave now."

"My mother was blackmailing you," Melody said. "And you killed her."

Joe stared at her for a moment. In the odd lighting, it was

impossible to read the expression on his face. "I don't know what you're talking about," he said eventually.

"What did she know about you?" Melody demanded.

"I've never done anything that anyone could blackmail me over," Joe replied. "I suspect there are others in this room who can't say the same, though."

"What happened to your mother?" Barry asked.

Joe spun around and glared at the man. "I don't talk about my mother," he snapped.

"You had to stay in Nightshade to look after her," Barry said. "And you hated that. You always said that as soon as something happened to her, you'd be on the next plane to Hollywood. And now she's been gone for over six years, and you're still here."

"I have a good job here. It would be foolish of me to give that up to chase an impossible dream."

"Was your mother really blackmailing people?" one of the guests asked Melody.

She shrugged. "I don't know anything for sure, but it's possible. She never told me where her money came from, but she often seemed to live above her means."

"As a lawyer, I think I should warn you to be very careful about what you say," another guest interjected.

Melody shook her head. "I want my mother's killer brought to justice. That's all that matters right now."

"We all want that," Joe said.

Melody stared at him. "You killed her, didn't you?"

Joe flushed and shook his head. "I barely knew your mother. We did a few shows together, but outside of that, we never really talked."

"That isn't true," Barry said. "You used to have lunch with her every Tuesday."

"We had lunch together once or twice," Joe admitted.

"It was every Tuesday," Barry said. "Helena said that you

used to take your mother out for lunch every Tuesday, and once she'd passed away, you found that you missed it. Helena was happy to take her place, going to the Lakeside with you every week."

"I remember that," Connie said. "Helena and I talked about it once. We were going to do some shopping one day, and she told me she couldn't do Tuesday afternoons because she spent every Tuesday with you."

"So we had lunch together once in a while," Joe said. "It hardly matters."

"What did you tell her?" Melody asked. "What secrets did you share with her?"

"I never told her anything. I don't have secrets," Joe said stiffly.

"It must have been something to do with his mother," Jessica said thoughtfully.

"You don't know?" Neal asked Melody. "Your mother didn't leave you a list of names and transgressions for which she was being paid?"

Melody shook her head. "If my mother had any such list, she kept it with her." She glanced at Greg and then looked back to Neal. "Not that there was any such list. Not that she was blackmailing anyone."

Neal chuckled. "My dear girl, she was blackmailing me. I'll admit to that much, but not to the why behind it all. It was a minor indiscretion and not a criminal one," he added, nodding at Greg.

"How much did you pay Helena over the years?" Ricky asked.

"Not much," Neal replied. "A small sum, remitted monthly, to a post office box. Not having to pay it any longer won't change my life, but I also won't miss sending it."

"I won't miss waiting for her to come back and demand more," Ricky said.

Everyone in the room turned to look at him.

"Helena was blackmailing you, too?" Connie asked.

Ricky flushed. "It wasn't a big deal," he muttered. "I told her something I should have kept to myself, that's all."

"And you've been paying for it for the last five years," Neal said.

Ricky nodded. "And worrying that she'd come back and demand more."

"She promised me that she'd never come back and never increase her demands," Neal said. "She said that once she left a town, she never went back."

"And you believed her?" Ricky asked.

Neal shrugged. "I hoped she was telling the truth. I did my best to put the whole thing out of my head, aside from sending her monthly payments, that is."

"She never would have come back," Melody told them. "She never revisited the same place twice, and she never asked anyone for more money."

"It sounds as if you knew a lot about all of this," Greg said.

"If you need a lawyer..." a guest began.

"Jeremy, hush," his wife interrupted.

Melody looked over at Joe. "How much did you pay my mother?" she asked.

"I didn't pay her anything. I barely knew her, and I certainly didn't tell her any of my secrets," he replied tightly.

"Or maybe you didn't pay her anything because you killed her when she tried to blackmail you," Jessica suggested.

Joe inhaled sharply. "What a ridiculous notion."

"It seems to me that everyone in here who has been sending money to my mother's post office box every month for the past five years has given themselves something of an alibi," Melody said. "Which means anyone who hasn't must move to the top of the suspect list."

THE BODY IN THE BOATHOUSE

"That makes it sound as if you think your mother was blackmailing everyone in town," Connie protested.

Melody stared at her for a moment. "Mom told me that everyone in the Nightshade Players had secrets. What was yours?"

Connie flushed and then looked down at the table. "I don't know what you're talking about."

"But you were paying my mother, weren't you?" Melody countered. "And that's a good thing, because it means you didn't kill her."

"Maybe the killer was smart enough to keep paying anyway," Joe suggested.

Melody laughed. "You want me to believe that because you killed her and you stopped paying. I don't think the police will have any trouble finding the evidence they need to put you behind bars now that they know exactly where to look."

"I didn't kill anyone," Joe exclaimed.

"Maybe the police should dig up your mother," Barry suggested.

Joe turned his head and glared at Barry. "How dare you!"

"That comment struck a nerve," Connie said.

Joe shouted something and then turned and raced toward the door. Greg ran after him as Joe pulled the door open and ran outside. A moment later Abigail heard the sound of the generator firing up. As lights came on around the room, she ran to the door.

Greg was standing at the bottom of the short flight of steps that led to the porch. Joe was on the ground holding his legs and swearing loudly.

"I've called for an ambulance," Greg told Abigail. "He jumped off the porch and landed badly. I think he may have broken both of his legs."

Abigail felt her knees go weak. Greg caught her arm.

"Are you okay?" he asked.

"Sure, I'm fine," she lied. "I'm just a bit overwhelmed."

Sirens seemed to be coming from every direction. Abigail went back inside and waited while Joe was taken away in an ambulance under police guard. Fred took photos of the knife on the floor before he carefully slid it into an evidence bag and sent it away with one of the uniformed officers. Then he took statements from everyone at the party.

"I'm sorry," Abigail told the guests before they were each led away to talk to the police.

"It isn't your fault," one of them replied.

"And it's definitely been a Halloween to remember," another added.

The guests were all asked to return to their rooms once they'd been interviewed. Eventually, Abigail found herself in the lobby with just Melody, Jessica, Carl, and Arnold.

"What did I miss?" Carl asked as the last of the guests left the room.

"Everything," Jessica told him. "Helena was blackmailing everyone in town and Joe killed her."

"Joe? He always seemed like such a nice guy," Carl replied.

"He killed his mother," Melody said. "That's the only thing that makes sense. My mother never should have tried to blackmail him over something that serious."

"I would suggest that blackmail is always a bad idea," Abigail said.

Melody shrugged. "She usually only did it over minor things, things that people wouldn't want known but that weren't criminal. She'd flirt with a guy until he made a pass, and then she'd threaten to tell his wife or girlfriend, that sort of thing. Usually, they'd happily pay her a small amount every month to keep the whole incident quiet."

"Or she'd learn people's secrets," Jessica said.

"Yeah, she was really good at that. She could get people to tell her things that they really shouldn't have ever talked about.

Again, though, it was never anything criminal. Just minor indiscretions."

"Like what?" Carl asked.

"Usually it was to do with affairs," Melody replied. "Sometimes someone might have made a mistake at work and gotten away with it or managed to get it blamed on someone else, but it was usually about sex. People do all sorts of dumb things and then they want to tell someone else how dumb they've been. Mom was a great listener."

"Until she started blackmailing you for what you'd told her," Carl said dryly.

Melody shrugged. "She never asked for much money, and she never actually told anyone anything, even if people stopped paying. It was just a way for her to supplement her income. She didn't have a proper retirement plan. This was all she had."

"And it got her killed," Jessica said softly.

"Let's just hope the police can find evidence that Joe killed her," Melody said.

Fred interviewed Arnold and then Carl before he took Jessica away.

"I'm sorry that I ruined your party," Melody said as Abigail began to stack empty plates and glasses onto a tray.

She shrugged. "Let's just hope that the police can sort everything out and that if Joe did kill your mother, they can find evidence to prove it."

"I miss her. She and I had our differences, but I loved her a lot."

"I'm sorry for your loss."

"At least now I know what happened to her. It isn't going to be easy, getting over her death, but at least I won't have to wonder where she is or what she's doing."

"What will you do now?"

"Go home and get on with my life. I may need a lawyer to sort out a few things, but I'll worry about that tomorrow."

After Fred took Melody away, Abigail got more serious about cleaning up the mess from the party. She made several trips to the kitchen, keeping her thoughts focused on what she was doing so that she wouldn't think about everything that had happened that evening. At some point, Arnold joined her and silently began to help.

"Ms. Clark? I'm ready for you now," Fred said twenty minutes later.

"Good night," Melody said as she walked past Abigail and out of the lodge.

Abigail followed Fred into the small office and sank down into the guest chair. He sat down behind the desk and smiled sympathetically at her.

"This wasn't the Halloween party you were planning," he said.

"No, not at all. I just have to hope that none of the guests write terrible reviews of the lodge based on what happened here tonight."

"Tell me what happened in your own words."

"And then you arrived," she concluded several minutes later.

"In the future, if anyone tells you that they're deliberately trying to set a trap for a killer with themselves as the bait, please call me," Fred said.

Abigail flushed. "I should have called you. I didn't expect her to be successful, really."

"Remember that we don't know that she has been successful. As of this moment, we've no evidence that Joe has done anything wrong."

"I saw him behind Melody with a knife, and he did try to run away."

"We'll be questioning him closely once he's able to speak to us. He's in surgery right now."

"Surgery?"

"I'll just say that he did quite a lot of damage to one of his legs when he jumped off the porch. Let's leave it at that."

Abigail sighed. "Do you think he killed Helena?"

"My job is to find evidence. What I think doesn't matter."

At least a dozen more questions sprang into Abigail's mind, but she ignored them all. Fred wasn't going to answer them and the last thing she wanted to do was annoy the man.

"I'll be back in the morning to talk to Melody again," he said as he got to his feet. "I don't expect her to stay in Nightshade for long now that she thinks the case is solved."

"I'll see you in the morning, then."

Abigail followed him to the door and then shut and locked it behind him.

"Go and get some sleep," Arnold said from behind her.

"I don't think I can sleep right now, but I suppose I should try."

Arnold pulled her into a tight hug. "It's going to be okay," he assured her.

"What if Melody was wrong about Joe?" she asked. "What if the person who really did kill her mother is still out there, waiting for a chance to kill Melody?"

"I don't think she was wrong about Joe. I think Joe killed his own mother and then made the mistake of admitting it to Helena. When Helena tried to blackmail him, he killed her."

Abigail shivered. "I may never sleep again."

Arnold walked her to her room in the annex and then waited while she let herself in.

"Good night," he said.

"Good night," she replied, shutting the door, locking it, and finally sliding a chair in front of the door. When she crawled into bed a short while later, she deliberately didn't look at the clock. It would be better if she didn't know how little sleep she was going to be able to get.

"It's morning," she said to Marcia the next morning.

Marcia handed her a cup of coffee.

Abigail took a sip and then sighed. "That's a little bit better, anyway."

"Melody isn't answering her door," Fred said as he stuck his head into the kitchen.

"Maybe she's just a sound sleeper," Abigail suggested as she followed the man into the lobby.

"Maybe she disappeared in the middle of the night," Fred countered.

Abigail grabbed her master key and then walked with Fred to the annex. She knocked loudly several times before using her key to open the door. The room was empty of everything except its furnishings.

"She even took your bedding," Fred commented as he surveyed the scene.

"And the towels," Abigail said as she looked into the bathroom.

Fred sighed. "I thought she'd stay long enough to make sure that Joe confessed."

"Did he?"

He hesitated and then nodded. "It will be all over the news later today. I talked to him this morning, and he confessed to everything. He said he couldn't keep quiet any longer, that guilt had been eating at him for too long and that he'd already ruined his life, so things couldn't get any worse."

"He admitted that he killed Helena?"

"I'm not going to say anything further. As I said, I'm sure it will be all over the news sites later."

Fred took another look around the empty hotel room and then sighed. "I'd be willing to bet that Melody didn't just disappear from here. I'm sure she's long gone, probably to start a new life in another country with all of her mother's ill-gotten gains."

"She did say something about retiring to Mexico."

"I'm not sure we can prove that she did anything illegal, even if she did know what her mother was doing." Fred sighed. "I'd better get back to the office and start writing up my reports."

Back at her desk, Abigail fired up her computer. "Local man admits to murdering two women," she read off the local news website.

"Joe has confessed, has he?" Arnold asked.

"It sounds like it." Abigail had only just started reading the article when the door opened and Jessica walked in.

"We've solved another one," she said happily.

"Melody nearly got stabbed," Abigail countered.

"But she didn't. I don't think Joe would have stabbed her, even though he probably really wanted to. He was just panicked and reacted without thinking."

"According to Carl, there was a lot of damage to the generator," Arnold said. "And he'd short-circuited the wiring somehow to make the power fail as well."

"All of that required quite a lot of thought," Abigail said.

Jessica shrugged. "All's well that ends well, then. Where is Melody?"

"She's gone. She disappeared in the middle of the night, taking all of the bedding and towels from her room when she went," Abigail replied.

Jessica grinned. "She'll be on her way to Mexico or maybe somewhere more exotic. She must have a considerable fortune tucked away somewhere."

Before Abigail could reply, the first of the guests came

down the stairs ready for their Sunday brunch. Jessica joined them and they all chatted together about their extraordinary Halloween evening.

"We'll be back for your next themed weekend," one of the guests assured Abigail as they headed back up to pack their things. "We had a wonderful time."

"I'm glad to hear that," Abigail replied. *Let's just hope next time there won't be any killers to unmask.*

The Body in the Cottage
A SUNSET LODGE MYSTERY

Release date: May 12, 2023

Abigail is delighted when her sister, Mandy, the co-owner of Sunset Lodge, arrives to spend a week with her. Both sisters are excited to finally have an opportunity to really talk about their plans for renovating, remodeling, and redecorating just about every inch of the main lodge building, the annex, and the cottages in the woods around the lodge. With a laser measure in one hand and a notebook in the other, Mandy wants to take notes on each of the cottages so that she can start sketching out her plans for their improvements.

The dead body in Cottage Four is an unexpected and unwelcome discovery. Abigail, who's already been through two murder investigations, wants to leave the detective work to the police, but Mandy is eager to start asking questions and talking to everyone in the small town of Nightshade.

As Mandy drags her sister around town, doing everything she can to throw them into the paths of various suspects,

THE BODY IN THE COTTAGE

Abigail knows that their neighbor, Jessica, is busy doing some snooping as well. All Abigail wants to do is get the lodge ready for a special Thanksgiving weekend, but instead she has to worry that a killer might target her neighbor or even her sister next.

A sneak peek at The Body in the Cottage

A Sunset Lodge Mystery
Release date: May 12, 2023

Please excuse any typos or minor errors. I have not yet completed final edits on this title.

Chapter One

"Mandy, I can't believe you're finally here," Abigail Clark said, pulling her sister into a tight hug.

"Me, too, either," Amanda Clark laughed. "Not that a burst pipe is a good thing, but I must admit I wasn't disappointed when the theater had to shut for a week. It gave me the perfect opportunity to come and spend time with my big sister, and to put in some serious hours of hard work here, since I'm supposed to be the co-owner of the lodge, and this is the first time I've been here since we toured it before we bought it."

"You've been busy."

"I have and it's been wonderful finally doing what I've

A SNEAK PEEK AT THE BODY IN THE COTTAGE

always dreamed of doing, designing and building sets for shows, even if the ones I've done aren't quite on Broadway."

"While I'm glad you're here, I wish you were going to be here for Thanksgiving."

"Me, too, but the theater will be back together again by Thanksgiving, and I'll be hard at work on the sets for the next show. Your plans for Thanksgiving weekend look wonderful, by the way."

"Thanks. I've been fine tuning them for ages, especially now that the weekend is sold out."

"You've sold out? How wonderful."

"We've sold out," Abigail corrected her. "Sunset Lodge is half yours."

"How many rooms have you sold, then?"

"All four on the second floor, three in the annex, and two on the third floor. I haven't had time to paint the other two rooms on the third floor, but I think nine rooms full of guests is enough for one weekend. I'm already getting stressed about it and it's still a couple of weeks away."

Mandy frowned. "I can try to get away."

"Don't be silly. You stay in New York City, working your dream job. I can manage here just fine. I used to manage much larger properties and their restaurants as well."

"Does this seem very different?"

"I can't even begin to tell you how different it feels. It feels completely different, knowing that we own the place. Before this, I'd always worked for someone else."

"But you're happy here, right?"

Abigail nodded. "I'd be happier if I hadn't found two dead bodies in the past two months, but I'm doing everything in my power to forget about all of that and focus on the good."

"You painted in here," Mandy said, looking around the lodge's large lobby.

A SNEAK PEEK AT THE BODY IN THE COTTAGE

"I did, with some help. We painted every room on this floor, all of the guest rooms on the second floor, and two of the guest rooms on the third floor. We also painted every room in the annex, but some of those rooms need a lot more than a coat of paint."

"I assume you aren't planning to use the room where the body was found again?"

"Not for guests, anyway. Not for anyone overnight. Right now, I'm using it for storage, but we may find another use for it eventually."

"Where am I staying?"

"You can stay anywhere you'd like. We don't have any guests coming this week. While our special Thanksgiving weekend sold out, as did our Halloween party weekend, I've struggled to get guests here at any other time. I really hope we aren't going to have to have special themed weekends all year long just get a few guests to visit."

"Things will pick up in the spring and summer," Mandy predicted. "What are you going to do about the boathouse?"

"I'm not certain. Barry isn't sure he wants to go in the boathouse, not after his former girlfriend was murdered in there, but I don't know if we'll be able to find anyone else to run boat rentals for us. Right now, the boathouse and rental business is at the bottom of my list of concerns, though. No one is going out on the lake for the next several months, not without ice skates, anyway."

"The lake isn't frozen already, is it?"

"No, but we've already had a dusting of snow and it's only going to get worse from here."

"Ah, I knew I heard voices, but I was waiting to get the cake out of the oven," a voice said from the doorway that led into the kitchen.

"Marcia, hello," Abigail said. "Mandy, this is Marcia

Burton, Sunset Lodge's brilliant chef, cook, baker, caterer, everything."

Marcia, a motherly-looking woman in her fifties, laughed. "I try. I've been cooking at Sunset Lodge for over twenty years, and I can't imagine doing anything else. I love to cook and now that you and your sister own the lodge, I'm getting to do all sorts of fun and interesting things."

"It's very nice to meet you," Mandy said. "Were you not allowed to have fun under the previous owners?"

"I didn't mean that, not exactly, but Jack and Janet had very definite ideas about how they wanted to lodge to operate. We had a set menu, and I made the same things on the various days of the weeks every week for, well, decades. I was allowed to do a bit more with breakfast, but I always had to have the same basics available. I'm not complaining. There were some advantages to keeping things simple, but I must admit that I'm really enjoying all of the things that your sister has let me do since she's been here."

"What have you been letting Marcia do?" Mandy asked Abigail.

"Anything she wants, really. I don't mind what she makes, especially when we don't have guests. When we do have guests, we need to let them know what to expect, but it certainly doesn't have to be the same menu every week. I also had her plan some fun, themed meals for Halloween."

"And she suggested that I could do the same for Thanksgiving weekend, but I don't think anyone should interfere with a traditional Thanksgiving feast," Marcia added.

Mandy nodded. "But you could do some interesting things on the day before and the day after."

"We're still talking about that," Marcia said. "I've been experimenting with a few different dishes."

"If you need a taste tester, I'm here all week," Mandy said.

Everyone laughed.

A SNEAK PEEK AT THE BODY IN THE COTTAGE

"And now I'm going to ask a dumb question," Mandy said. "I know we toured the property before we bought it, but we never met any of the staff back then. Abigail said something about you living in a cottage nearby. Is that right?"

"That's exactly right. The lodge owns eight cottages altogether," Marcia told her. "Jack and Janet used four of them for guests. They're scattered through the small forest around the lodge. On the very edge of the property there are three cottages in a small cluster. That's where all of the staff live."

"All of the staff?" Mandy echoed questioningly.

"I live in the nicest of the cottages," Marcia said, grinning. "I live with my husband, Howard. It's just the two of us now that our children are off on their own. They grew up in that cottage, and they still stay with when they come back to town, which isn't very often, sadly."

"Carl Young lives in the smallest of the three," Abigail said. "He's single and he's been living there and working here for something like thirty years."

Marcia nodded. "And Arnold and Karen Nagel live in the third. He's the night manager here."

"Got it. Four guest cottages, three staff cottages, but didn't you say there were eight altogether?" Mandy asked.

"There's another cottage on the other side of the property. Jack and Janet thought it was too far from the lodge to use for guests. We were all given the option of living there when we first came to work for the lodge, but Carl and Arnold and I all preferred to live close to one another. I believe Jack and Janet just used that cottage for storage."

Abigail nodded. "I remember them telling us about it when we first toured the property, but then I promptly forgot about it. It's quite far from the lodge building and I'm sure Jack told me that it wasn't really habitable."

"I certainly wouldn't put guests in there," Marcia said. "At one point, when Jack and Janet were having some difficulties, she threatened to move herself out there, but in the end she decided she's rather stay where she was."

"Have you done anything with the owner's suite?" Mandy asked her sister.

Abigail shook her head. "I've been staying in the annex. While the rooms out there need a lot of updating, the owner's suite needs – actually I'm not sure what it needs, but whatever it is, it isn't going to be cheap."

Mandy laughed. "Of course, we didn't really get a very good look at it when we took our tour. Jack and Janet were still living there."

"Now it's empty and you can see just how much work it needs," Abigail said. "Carpets, paint, and a new bathroom to start. There's a small kitchenette, too, but I unplugged the appliances. I think they're all older than I am."

Marcia nodded. "Nothing in that suite has been touched in all the years I've been here, and I remember Janet complaining about how old everything was up there when I was first hired. She tried to talk Jack into replacing the bathroom for years until she finally gave up. She also used to try to convince him to take out the kitchenette, because she said they never used it. Jack needed the refrigerator for his beer, though, and he used the microwave for popcorn and sometimes to reheat leftovers from my kitchen."

"Leftovers from your kitchen?" Abigail repeated, puzzled.

"Sometimes guests would skip meals even though I'd been expecting them. Jack hated to see food go to waste, so when that happened, he'd take the extra food put to their suite and then reheat for lunch or dinner the next day," Marcia explained.

"I suppose that makes sense. We haven't really had that problem since I've been here as we've only had a handful of guests."

"And your sister has been kind enough to let me take

whatever leftovers we have had home to Howard," Marcia told Mandy.

"That seems fair enough," Mandy said. "But now I'm curious about the extra cottage. We didn't see that one when we toured, did we?"

Abigail shook her head. "Like I said, I forgot it was even out there. It's on the very edge of the property."

"Let's go and take a look," Mandy suggested. "I want to look at all of the cottages while I'm here. I'm going to take some measurements so I can start planning their themes."

"You're here for a week. We don't have to go through the cottages today."

"But the sooner we do, the sooner I can get started on my sketches. And once those are finished, you can start on the work that needs to be done in order to bring my ideas to life."

Abigail laughed. "I'm excited to see your ideas, but I don't think we have the money right now to start remodeling the cottages. If I remember correctly, they're all going to need a lot of work. We may have to gut them all and start from scratch."

"I don't think they're that bad," Marcia said. "The one closest to the lodge was updated about five years ago. Jack and Janet had the bathroom completely redone and they added a whirlpool tub. They replaced all the carpeting and painted the walls and then put in all new furniture. The only thing wrong with it now is a bit of neglect. They stopped renting it out about two years ago when Janet decided that getting back and forth to the cottages to clean them was too much work."

Abigail nodded. "I remember that one being in fairly good condition, but I wasn't a huge fan of the paint colors."

Mandy laughed. "Is that the one that was all bright pink and pale purple with hearts painted on every wall?"

"That's the one," Abigail said.

"When they added the whirlpool tub, they thought it

might appeal to honeymooners and couples looking for a romantic getaway," Marcia explained. "As it happened, it was most popular with married women who came and stayed by themselves for a few days away from their kids. They loved the big, deep tub and that they could soak for hours and not be interrupted."

Abigail and Mandy laughed.

"I can see that," Mandy said. "Maybe, if I ever get married and have children, I'll hide in that cottage, too. Or maybe it would be better if we did something similar to the cottage on the other side of the property. Not the pink and purple hearts, of course, but maybe we could turn that cottage into the nicest one of them all."

Abigail sighed. "You aren't going to be happy until you've seen that cottage, are you?"

"You said yourself that you haven't seen it. We really ought to inspect everything that's ours now."

"Yes, but the last time I did something similar, I stumbled across a skeleton. I'm sure you can understand why I'm less excited than you are about exploring another building that hasn't been unlocked for years."

"We aren't going to find another dead body," Mandy said. "But if you truly don't want to visit the cottage, you don't have to. Just give me the key."

Abigail sighed. "We can go and take a look at the cottage. I suppose we don't have anything else to do this afternoon."

"And while we're out there, we may as well visit all of the cottages," Mandy suggested.

"I suppose we may as well."

"The cottages were always very popular with guests," Marcia said. "Before Jack and Janet decided that cleaning them was too much work and they stopped renting them out, I mean."

"They all have kitchenettes, don't they?" Mandy asked.

"Do you think that was part of their attraction, because I'd really like to get rid of them. There isn't any way to make kitchen appliances attractive."

Marcia laughed. "I'm not sure how much the kitchenettes mattered to our guests. We still did breakfast and dinner every day for guests in the cottages, so it wasn't as if they were doing a lot of cooking out there. I do know that some appreciate having refrigerators for cold drinks. Guests in the cottages often used to ask for leftovers, too, in case they got hungry again during the night, but Jack and Janet didn't allow me to give the guests food to take back to the cottages."

"Why not?" Mandy asked.

"I think they were afraid it might encourage the guests in the main building to ask for food to take back to their rooms. They hated it when people ate in the rooms in the main lodge."

"So you don't provide room service," Mandy laughed.

"No, never. Meals are served in the dining room and nowhere else."

"And I'm not planning to change that," Abigail said. "I might be a bit more flexible about things like letting guests in the cottages take food back from dinner, but I'd rather guests didn't eat in the rooms in the lodge, too."

"What about snacks? I mean, I might just want a small snack or two while I'm here," Mandy said.

Abigail laughed. "You own half of the lodge. You can do whatever you want, but you have to clean up your own mess."

"That sounds fair."

"For now, let's go and look at cottages, shall we?"

Mandy nodded. "Thanks, Big Sister. I'll just drop my suitcase somewhere. Where should I put it?"

"Why don't you stay in one of the second-floor rooms? They're the most comfortable rooms we have and they're all clean and ready for guests."

"Where are you staying now?"

"I'm out in the annex."

"Then I'll stay in the annex, next door to you."

Abigail chuckled. "You may regret that decision. The annex rooms aren't nearly as nice as the rooms in here."

"So why are you staying out there?"

"Because they're adequate for my needs and because I want to leave the rooms in here ready for guests. Imagine if a large group suddenly arrived and I had to tell them they could have rooms, just as soon as I moved out of one of them?"

Mandy chuckled. "Surely it isn't any better if you have to tell them that your sister needs to move out."

"I suppose not. Okay, you can stay in the annex. We can both feel foolish about leaving rooms empty for guests who are never actually going to arrive."

Abigail crossed to the reception desk and opened the small safe behind it. She pulled out the box of keys and found the right key for Mandy, then she pulled out the small, zippered bag that contained the keys to the cottages. She checked that the keys for the four guest cottages were in the bag and then pulled out the key labelled "Storage Cottage."

"All set?" Mandy asked.

"I think so," Abigail replied as she slipped the bag of keys into her coat pocket.

"Dinner will be ready in two hours," Marcia said.

"Excellent. What are we having for dinner?" Mandy asked.

"I'm doing a test run on our Thanksgiving meal, actually," Marcia told her. "So it's turkey with all the trimmings."

"Oh, delicious," Mandy said.

"You'll have a chance to meet Arnold and Carl at dinner," Abigail said.

"I'm looking forward to it."

"I'm going to lock the front door so no one can wander in unannounced," Abigail told Marcia.

"I'm sure Carl or Arnold could watch reception," Marcia said.

"It's fine. I'll put the note on the door with my cell number. If an unexpected guest suddenly arrives, he or she can call me." She looked at Mandy. "Follow me, then. I'll show you to your room."

The pair walked out of the main lodge building. Abigail stopped to lock the door behind them before hanging the small sign with her cell number on it on the small hook in the center of the door.

"Do you always have to do that?" Mandy asked.

"I try to stay behind the reception desk for most of the day. When I do have other things to do, then, yes, I usually lock the door and put up the sign."

"Running the lodge is a demanding job."

"It is, but I'm happy here."

"I'm glad to hear that, although it doesn't make me feel any less guilty about not being here."

"I don't want to hear another word about that," Abigail said firmly as she led her sister around to the annex. She opened a door and then handed her sister the key. "Your new home, for the week, anyway."

Mandy walked into the small room and looked around. "I've stayed in much worse places."

Abigail laughed. "That isn't exactly high praise."

"I think we should work on some sort of theme for the annex, too, but the cottages are probably more important."

"I think so. Ideally, I'd prefer guests in the main lodge building first, but if that's full, the cottages would be my next choice, once they're ready to use. Come spring, we should be able to charge a lot more for one of the cottages than we can for a room in this annex."

Mandy nodded and then pulled a small notebook out of one of her bags. "So let's get to work on the cottages." She went in another bag and pulled out something else. "I'm ready to go."

"What is that?"

"A laser measuring device. It's a lot easier than trying to use a tape measure. I need accurate measurements if I'm going to plan themes."

Abigail smiled. "Just remember that we don't actually have any money in the budget for remodeling right now. I'm happy for you to start planning, but it may be years before we can afford to put all of your plans into action."

"That's fine," Mandy said with a wave of her hand. "For now, I just want to see all of the cottages."

Also by Diana Xarissa

The Sunset Lodge Mysteries

The Body in the Annex
The Body in the Boathouse
The Body in the Cottage

The Lady Elizabeth Cozies in Space

Alibis in Alpha Sector
Bodies in Beta Sector

The Midlife Crisis Mysteries

Anxious in Nevada
Bewildered in Florida

The Isle of Man Ghostly Cozy Mysteries

Arrivals and Arrests
Boats and Bad Guys
Cars and Cold Cases
Dogs and Danger
Encounters and Enemies
Friends and Frauds
Guests and Guilt
Hop-tu-Naa and Homicide

Invitations and Investigations

Joy and Jealousy

Kittens and Killers

Letters and Lawsuits

Marsupials and Murder

Neighbors and Nightmares

Orchestras and Obsessions

Proposals and Poison

Questions and Quarrels

Roses and Revenge

Secrets and Suspects

Theaters and Threats

Umbrellas and Undertakers

Visitors and Victims

Weddings and Witnesses

Xylophones and X-Rays

The Isle of Man Cozy Mysteries

Aunt Bessie Assumes

Aunt Bessie Believes

Aunt Bessie Considers

Aunt Bessie Decides

Aunt Bessie Enjoys

Aunt Bessie Finds

Aunt Bessie Goes

Aunt Bessie's Holiday

Aunt Bessie Invites

Aunt Bessie Joins
Aunt Bessie Knows
Aunt Bessie Likes
Aunt Bessie Meets
Aunt Bessie Needs
Aunt Bessie Observes
Aunt Bessie Provides
Aunt Bessie Questions
Aunt Bessie Remembers
Aunt Bessie Solves
Aunt Bessie Tries
Aunt Bessie Understands
Aunt Bessie Volunteers
Aunt Bessie Wonders
Aunt Bessie's X-Ray
Aunt Bessie Yearns
Aunt Bessie Zeroes In

The Aunt Bessie Cold Case Mysteries

The Adams File
The Bernhard File
The Carter File
The Durand File
The Evans File
The Flowers File
The Goodman File
The Howard File

The Markham Sisters Cozy Mystery Novellas

The Appleton Case

The Bennett Case

The Chalmers Case

The Donaldson Case

The Ellsworth Case

The Fenton Case

The Green Case

The Hampton Case

The Irwin Case

The Jackson Case

The Kingston Case

The Lawley Case

The Moody Case

The Norman Case

The Osborne Case

The Patrone Case

The Quinton Case

The Rhodes Case

The Somerset Case

The Tanner Case

The Underwood Case

The Vernon Case

The Walters Case

The Xanders Case

The Young Case

The Zachery Case

The Janet Markham Bennett Cozy Thrillers

The Armstrong Assignment
The Blake Assignment
The Carlson Assignment
The Doyle Assignment
The Everest Assignment
The Farnsley Assignment
The George Assignment
The Hamilton Assignment

The Isle of Man Romances

Island Escape
Island Inheritance
Island Heritage
Island Christmas

The Later in Life Love Stories

Second Chances
Second Act
Second Thoughts
Second Degree
Second Best
Second Nature
Second Place

Bookplates Are Now Available

Would you like a signed bookplate for this book?

I now have bookplates (stickers) that I can personalize, sign, and send to you. It's the next best thing to getting a signed copy!

Send an email to diana@dianaxarissa.com with your mailing address (I promise not to use it for anything else, ever) and how you'd like your bookplate personalized and I'll sign one and send it to you.

There is no charge for a bookplate, but there is a limit of one per person.

About the Author

Diana has been self-publishing since 2013, and she feels surprised and delighted to have found readers who enjoy the stories and characters that she imagines. Always an avid reader, she still loves nothing more than getting lost in fictional worlds, her own or others!

After being raised in Erie, Pennsylvania, and studying history at Allegheny College in Meadville, Pennsylvania, Diana pursued a career in college administration. She was living and working in Washington, DC, when she met her future husband, an Englishman who was visiting the city.

Following her marriage, Diana moved to Derbyshire. A short while later, she and her husband relocated to the Isle of Man. After ten years on the island, during which Diana earned a Master's degree in the island's history, they made the decision to relocate again, this time to the US.

Now living near Buffalo, New York, Diana and her husband live with their daughter, a student at the University at Buffalo. Their son is now living and working just outside of Boston, Massachusetts, giving Diana an excuse to travel now and again.

Diana also writes mystery/thrillers set in the not-too-distant future as Diana X. Dunn and Young Adult fiction as D.X. Dunn.

She is always happy to hear from readers. You can write to her at:

Diana Xarissa Dunn
PO Box 72
Clarence, NY 14031.

Find Diana at: DianaXarissa.com
E-mail: Diana@dianaxarissa.com